AVARICE

Gripping Scottish detective crime fiction

PETE BRASSETT

Paperback published by The Book Folks

London, 2017

© Pete Brassett

ISBN 978-1-5207-0589-7

www.thebookfolks.com

AVARICE is the second novel by Pete Brassett to feature detectives Munro and West. Look out for SHE, the first book, and ENMITY, DUPLICITY, TERMINUS, TALION, and PERDITION, all of which can be enjoyed on their own, or as a series.

Chapter 1

Another irate customer pushed the door, cupped his hands against the grimy glass and peered inside. The antiquated finisher, with its worn sanding belts and tired brushes, stood idle in the gloom. Wooden implements lay scattered across the workbench, an apron hung from the iron jack and rows of unclaimed shoes lined the racks against the wall. He checked his watch: 3pm, just after. Too late for lunch and too early, surely, to close for the day. He noticed the sign in the window, a half-hearted affair scribbled in black marker pen on a large piece of scuffed cardboard framed with silver gaffer tape. "Closed from 11th to 24th. Please collect all shoes by 10th." He pulled his phone from his pocket and checked the date. It was Tuesday 10th and the cobbler was nowhere to be seen. The customer cursed. It wasn't the first time he'd been caught out, nor was it likely to be the last. A furious young lady, glowering with rage, stormed towards him, glanced inside the shop and rattled the door. She swore under her breath before demanding to know if he'd seen 'Rudy'. The man held up the receipt for his loafers and shook his head apologetically.

* * *

Ruben 'Rudy' Kappelhoff was, to the envy of many a man half his age, too fit, too healthy and, with his rugged complexion, too handsome for a sixty-year-old. He sat on the grass, bike by his side, his grey sweatshirt drenched with perspiration and gazed out across the Firth of Clyde. A brisk breeze tousled his mop of thick, white hair as he swigged Machrie Moor from a pewter hip flask. He ranted under his breath, bemoaning the haughty, supercilious dunderheads who plagued his shop with cheap but fashionable shoes held together with nothing more than a good dollop of optimism.

He was one of a dying breed and, to all intents and purposes, peerless. His only competition, if they could be regarded as such, was a kiosk located on the lower-ground floor of a shopping mall approximately six miles away. Unlike his rivals, a franchised chain whose reputation was built on speedy repairs using inferior stock, Rudy was a traditionalist, a professional, a craftsman with a faultless attention to detail.

As a young man in Dörpling, where he'd honed his skills under the watchful eye of his father, he'd learned that the best reward for his efforts was not the cash that lined his pockets, but the gleaming smiles of gratitude from the farmhands and labourers upon whose boots he'd bestowed a new lease of life.

Unfortunately, his diligence in repairing shoes was in pitiful supply when it came to time-keeping which, much to the annoyance of his faithful customers, could be described, at best, as erratic and unreliable. Although the sign on the door, faded and yellow, proclaimed his opening hours to be 9.30am – 5.30pm, Monday to Saturday, everyone knew it was for decoration only and not to be taken seriously. Depending on his mood, he might work for an hour or two one day, eighteen hours straight the next, but then again, some days, he may not turn up at all.

The ensuing barrage of abuse from disgruntled

customers when he did eventually resurface was not a cause for concern. He was hardened to it and, once he'd explained, at length, in his lilting Teutonic brogue, the reason for his tardiness, their ire would turn to compassion.

The small workshop, though well-ventilated, was a toxic environment in which to ply his trade. The fumes from the volatile polychloroprene adhesive would bring on bouts of dizziness and make him drowsy, the compound irritated his skin and was prone to making his eyes water, and the microscopic particles of rubber and leather that filled the air choked his lungs till he could scarcely breathe. As a consequence, for the sake of his health, he had no choice but to rest and recuperate, which invariably involved riding his bicycle from dawn till dusk, his head wrapped in his trademark bandana, his brow furrowed with a steely determination.

It was, as an excuse, as viable as any other, but some of his clients, and most of the locals, chose to subscribe to one of many alternative theories for his vagarious behaviour. There was, for example, the rumour that the real reason for his punishing excursions along the craggy, Greenock Cut to Cauldron Hill was to work off the hangovers. That he was, in fact, a recovering alcoholic who frequently jumped off the wagon and that his battle with the bottle was the result of an acrimonious divorce decades earlier. Though his wife had cited 'unreasonable behaviour' and 'irreconcilable differences' as the reasons for the split, he could, apparently, have counter-filed citing adultery, but chose not to, despite the fact he knew she'd been having an affair for a full four months prior to their separation. He'd become, quite frankly, sick of the sight of her. Then there were those who claimed the scars, one of which ran the length of his left forearm, the other around the back of his neck, were not the result of an industrial accident, but the legacy of an altercation with a border guard in his homeland for which he'd served a ten-stretch, guilty of a crime that fell somewhere between ABH and manslaughter. And then there were the few, those who daren't venture near his shop, who, based on his vociferous outbursts during which he'd launch a tirade of abuse against anyone in a position of authority, or those who held views opposed to his own, claimed he'd fled Germany not because he'd been persecuted for his faith, but because he'd absconded from a psychiatric hospital. Fortunately for Rudy, the rumours were based on malicious gossip and hearsay rather than fact, and, as the older folk in the village knew, flew in the face of his otherwise placid disposition.

He pulled a sandwich from his knapsack, corned beef, sauerkraut and cheese crammed between two slices of rye bread, and contemplated the view towards Innellan, blissfully unaware of the kerfuffle outside his shop.

Chapter 2

The dog, a black, Flat-Coated Retriever, sat patiently by his owner in the dappled, morning sunlight as the Daff, swollen by the previous night's rainfall, coursed its way through the glen, cascading over the smooth, rocky outcrops, bouncing off the banks and surging across the legs of the partially submerged body lying face down in the mud. It barked approvingly as Sergeant Iain Campbell, soaked to the waist, dragged the sodden weight from the icy water to the riverbank and gently rolled it over. He checked for a pulse, lowered his face to hers and felt a short, shallow breath on his cheek.

'You hold on, now,' he whispered, 'soon have you out of here, just you hold on.'

Her eyes, hollow and lifeless, blinked in acknowledgement. Her skin, soft and puffy, had turned the palest shade of blue but, most alarmingly, she did not shiver. Assuming she was on the brink of death, he pulled off his jacket and laid it over her chest.

'Watch yourself!' he yelled, as a paramedic scrambled through the maze of birch and alder towards him. 'It's slippery down here. Ambulance?'

'Right behind me,' said the medic, placing his middle

finger on her neck. 'She's alive. Just. Is this where you found her?'

'Near enough,' said Campbell.

'So you've moved her?'

'Aye, not much, she was…'

'Numpty. We'll have to stretcher her out, mind your back.'

Campbell stood aside as the paramedic, assisted by the ambulance crew, placed an oxygen mask over her mouth, strapped her onto a spinal board and hauled her away. Inspector McGreevy was waiting at the top of the embankment.

'Iain, Christ, you're soaked,' he said. 'What've you got?'

'Pneumonia, if I'm lucky,' said Campbell, buttoning his tunic. 'Female, chief, mid-fifties, I reckon. 5'6", thereabouts, dark-blonde hair, she's a bash to the back of the head. Looks like she slipped and fell, knocked herself out.'

'Not the smartest thing to do,' said McGreevy, 'trying to cross the river here, especially after that downpour.'

'Aye, you're not wrong, would've been dark, too,' said Campbell, 'probably couldn't see straight. Either way, it's not looking good, she's gone a funny colour.'

'Who found her?'

'Fella with the doggie, about a half an hour ago.'

'Did he call the ambulance?'

'No,' said Campbell, 'he thought she was dead. I called it in soon as I got here.'

'Well done. Anything else?'

'Constable Reid's along the bank there, to see if he can find a handbag or something.'

'Nothing to identify her?' said McGreevy.

'No, we'll have to wait till she gets to the hospital. I'll follow just as soon as I've changed into something a wee bit drier.'

'Okay, on your way, then. I'll make sure Duncan gets

a statement from yon dog lover, then we'll cordon this place off, get a proper search underway.'

* * *

'Can I get you something, Sergeant?' said the nurse, with a sympathetic tilt of the head. 'Cup of coffee, maybe? Warm you up?'

'No thanks, hen,' said Campbell with an appreciative smile, 'I'm fine.'

'Sure? It's no bother.'

'Really.'

'Okay, I'll just close these curtains and leave you to it. Shame she didn't…'

'Aye, I'm sure you did your best.'

Campbell, cap in hand, stared at the nameless corpse lying beneath a thin, cotton sheet; the hair still wet, the eyes closed, the face a ghostly pallor.

'Sergeant Campbell?'

'Aye, you must be…'

'Doctor Clark. Andy. Sorry we couldn't… it was a big ask, considering.'

'Right enough,' said Campbell, 'so, what do you…?'

Clark held up a sealed, plastic bag containing a small, leather wallet and a gold necklace.

'First of all, this is for you,' he said.

'Is that it?' said Campbell, surprised. 'No keys, cash, phone maybe?'

'Nope. But the wallet might help, there's a couple of cards in there. At least you'll have a name to go on.'

'Okay, thanks. What about her clothes? We might need to…'

'That brings me to my next point,' said Clark. 'She's still wearing them. Probably best to wait until the pathologist has finished up.'

'Pathologist?'

'Aye. The bash to the head, I don't believe that came from a fall and it looks like there's some damage to the eyes too, so no death certificate, I'm afraid. I've referred it

7

to the Procurator Fiscal for a post-mortem.'

'The Fiscal?' said Campbell. 'So, you reckon someone gave her a wee whack, then?'

'Maybe,' said Clark, with a despondent shake of the head, 'but I doubt that would have killed her, more likely to be the hypothermia but even then, there'd have to be some other contributing factors, something that may have expedited the onset. Look, I'll explain later, the Fiscal's giving us twenty minutes out of her lunch break, is that okay with you?'

'Aye, reckon so.'

'Good. McGreevy, will he come? He should be there.'

'Oh aye, wouldn't miss it for the world.'

'Right, see you there. Half an hour.'

'Half an... Christ, okay, I'll call him now.'

Clark stopped and turned as he left the cubicle.

'By the way,' he said, 'she whispered something before she passed away, sounded like "Lorna, tell Lorna", just so's you know.'

* * *

Isobel Crawford, unnaturally youthful for a fifty-three-year old with a penchant for red wine, Macallan single malt and Sobranie cocktail cigarettes, sat behind her cluttered desk and beckoned the entourage to sit.

'So, gentlemen,' she said, glancing at the unopened tuna sandwich before her, 'enlighten me before I starve to death. Who found the body?'

'That would be myself,' said Sergeant Campbell. 'Daff Glen. She was face down on the riverbank, half in the burn.'

'Anything suspicious?'

'Only the foolishness of trying to cross the river at night, looks like she fell and bashed her head, but the doctor here thinks otherwise.'

'Is that so?' said Crawford. 'Well, come on Mr. Clark, I'm always up for a good mystery. What's your professional opinion then?'

'Well,' said Clark, sighing as though he'd just finished a twelve-hour shift, 'there's a couple of things. First, I think the probable cause of death was exposure, but that's not conclusive, see, even if she was in the water for a few hours, she shouldn't have succumbed so readily, not unless she'd had a skinful, for example. Second, the reaction in her eyes when I examined her was not what I'd have expected, the response was negligible, like there's some nerve damage, perhaps. Also, the pupils were constricted. That's not normal. Finally, the injury to the back of her head; it's not consistent with a fall, not for someone of her size and build, the damage is too severe.'

'I see,' said Crawford, 'the mystery deepens. So, what do you want?'

'Post mortem,' said Clark.

'Very well, granted. How long will it take?'

'Oh, an hour or two, I imagine. No more. It's scheduled for this evening.'

'Annoyingly efficient. So, let's meet again in the morning, 8am. Oh, Inspector, I shall expect your report as well, is that okay?'

'Aye, nae bother, Isobel.'

'Good. Perhaps you'd like to bring some breakfast, too.'

* * *

McGreevy, agitated by the fact that the case would inevitably become a criminal inquiry, hovered uneasily by his car.

'Are you coming, chief?' said Campbell. 'I need to eat something. Soon.'

'Iain, here a wee moment,' said McGreevy, opening the door. 'If Doctor Clark finds something untoward as a result of the autopsy, you know what will happen, don't you?'

'Aye. CID will take over. We're not detectives, chief. After all, it is their job.'

'Right enough,' said McGreevy, with a sigh. 'Do you

not remember the last time they came to Gourock? How they took over the building? Your desk, and mine? Got blootered every evening and generally made a fool of themselves?'

'Not easy to forget.'

'Exactly, and with the Kip Regatta coming up next week, just the thought of it gives me the heebie jeebies. The place is already filling up with tourists, the last thing we need…'

'I ken what you're saying, chief, but what can we…?'

'I've an idea Iain, I only hope Isobel agrees to it. Grab yourself some lunch, I'll be a wee while.'

Chapter 3

McGreevy felt a pang of jealousy as he crawled along the narrow lane, one eye on the road, the other on the view across the Solway, the low sun bouncing off the water, the only sound, that of herring gulls squawking overhead, and, though the idea was appealing, wondered if he could actually ever settle in a place as quiet as Carsethorn. As dead as Carsethorn. He parked opposite a whitewashed, terraced cottage, thankful for the plume of grey smoke billowing from the chimney, a sign that someone was home.

A sprightly figure, tall and lean, clad in a green, waterproof hiking jacket and carrying a cane, marched purposefully towards him, paused at the gate and stared until a look of recognition crossed his face.

'If you're here to tell me they're stopping my pension,' said Munro, as McGreevy stepped from the car, 'you can leave now.'

'You're looking well, James. Not lost your sense of humour, then?'

'Never had one,' said Munro. 'What brings you down here? Is your sat-nav broken?'

'No, no. I was just passing,' said McGreevy, 'thought

I'd…'

'Just passing? 200 miles from home along a dead end street? You'd best come in, at least sit down before I say no to whatever it is you're after.'

The sitting room was comfortably, though not excessively furnished: a single armchair by the fire, a sofa pushed against the wall, a writing desk by the window, an oak sideboard, a standard lamp and a handful of books atop a single shelf.

'This is cosy, James,' said McGreevy, taking in the view from the window, 'are you comfortable here?'

'Aye, very.'

'I suppose what I mean is, do you not get a wee bit, lonely? Without Jean?'

'Oh, she's still here, Nick,' said Munro, thumping his chest, 'right here.'

McGreevy smiled, touched by the sentiment.

'Well, I have to say life down here obviously suits you, you do look…'

'Rejuvenated?' said Munro. 'Aye. I think that's the word I'd use, rejuvenated. No stress, no anger, no frustration. It's like a whole, new world. Now, will you take drink?'

'Well, I wouldn't say no…'

'I've a twelve-year old in here, somewhere,' said Munro, rummaging in the sideboard, 'as mellow as … och no, what am I saying, you're driving.'

'Yes, but…'

'And you're a police officer.'

'I know, but…'

'And you're on duty.'

'Aye, but surely just the one…'

'Milk and sugar?'

'If I must,' said McGreevy, with a sigh. 'If I must.'

Munro returned with two mugs of steaming strong tea, sat with satisfied sigh and opened a tin of shortbread.

'Don't hold back,' he said, as McGreevy helped

himself to a biscuit, 'I dare say you've not had your lunch, yet. So, tell me now, what is it you're after exactly?'

'Oh, nothing much,' said McGreevy, sheepishly, 'I was, I was just wondering what you had planned for tomorrow?'

'Tomorrow?' said Munro. 'Well, as it happens, I'm going take myself a walk, up the Criffel, if the weather holds out, that is.'

'Criffel? Is that not a bit, energetic?'

'Energetic? It's only 1800 feet, a wee hill. Why don't you join me? Shouldnae bother a man of your physical prowess.'

'It would bother me tremendously, James,' said McGreevy. 'Let's just say, I prefer the ground beneath my feet to be, level. No, see here, the thing is, I was going to ask you if you'd like to join me.'

'Oh, aye? It's not a round of golf you're talking about, is it?' said Munro, smirking.

'No.'

'More than likely a body of sorts.'

'Could be.'

'Probably unidentified.'

'Possibly.'

'With no obvious cause of death.'

'No yet.'

'No. Thanks for the offer,' said Munro, 'but I think a walk sounds more appealing, particularly to those of us who are retired.'

'Och, come on James, help me out here,' said McGreevy, 'I need someone who knows the area, someone who knows what they're doing. If you turn me down, the lads from Greenock will be all over the shop and there's the boat race coming up, too. Look, there's a nice wee hotel, generous expenses, I'll even…'

'Have you cleared this with the Fiscal?' said Munro.

'Well, no, no, not yet, but I will.'

Munro stood, walked to the window and, hands

clasped behind his back, stared out to sea.

'Will I have help?' he said.

McGreevy allowed himself a wry smile, confident that Munro was coming around.

'Of course,' he said, enthusiastically, 'there's Sergeant Campbell, he's years of experience, and young Duncan, that is, Constable Reid, you'll not meet a more enthusiastic…'

'No, no, no,' said Munro, shaking his head. 'I'll need someone who's a nose for this, no offence, Nick, but your lads simply aren't qualified for the job.'

'So, what are you saying?'

Munro paused before answering.

'I'll sleep on it,' he said, 'if I agree, I'll be in Gourock by 12 o'clock tomorrow.'

'And if you don't?'

'I'll be atop yon hill.'

* * *

Munro watched McGreevy's car fade to the distance, pulled the curtains tight and pokered up the fire. He sat for a moment and flicked through the newspaper he'd already read, took the mugs to the kitchen, opened the fridge, peered inside, and closed it again. The photo on the mantel shelf caught his eye. '*I know, Jean,*' he said, his shoulders slumping with the weight of the sigh, '*I know, but look at me, I'm that brain-dead, I'm talking to a wee photo. I mean, there's only so much walking a man can do, you understand, don't you? I'll not be long. I promise.*'

* * *

The early morning cloud, as black as pitch and heavy with the prospect of another downpour, rolled menacingly overhead as Munro tossed a holdall into the boot and left Carsethorn. Forsaking the monotony of the motorway for the longer but more scenic route north towards the coast, he drove at a leisurely pace usually employed by visitors in search of a castle ruin or a café serving square sausage and haggis toasties. By the time he'd reached Ardrossan, the cloud had given way to sun with glorious views across to Arran. Munro's knuckles turned white as he slammed on the brakes and slewed the car to the side of the road. '*Come on,*' he muttered as he frantically pulled his phone from his pocket and called a number he'd not used since leaving London, '*be there.*' It went straight to voicemail.

'*This is Charlotte. I'm away at the moment but if it's urgent, you can reach me on 01770 302302, but only if it's urgent. Bye.*'

Munro cursed and dialled.

'Hello?' he said, irritated by the poor reception, 'I don't mean to sound rude but, who is this?'

'Why, it's the Holy Isle.'

'Bingo!' said Munro. 'Listen, I wonder, would you happen to have a Miss Charlotte West staying with you? She's a friend, she said she may be…'

'Miss West? Aye, we did have, but I'm afraid you've missed her.'

'Missed her? When did she…'

'Just this morning.'

'This morning? Where to?'

'Back to the mainland, of course. The ferry, to Ardrossan.'

'And would you happen to know what time it…'

'Well, she was aboard the first one out, so all being well, it should have docked about, oh, a quarter of an hour ago.'

* * *

Munro, perched on the bonnet of his car, watched as a lone straggler, one of the last to disembark, ambled wearily along the gangway weighed down by the rucksack on her back. She was not the Detective Sergeant West he'd left behind in London. This one was gaunt and pale, like some starving waif from the wilderness who'd not eaten in days. She paused at the gates and looked around, pondering which direction to take, when her gaze eventually met his.

'Taxi?' he said, beaming broadly.

West regarded him with a look of utter surprise and grinned.

'D.I. James Munro! What the fuck are you doing here?' she said, quickening her pace. 'How did you…'

'You mentioned you might, you know, a while back, before I left, and I just happened to… how are you, Charlie?'

'Been better,' said West. 'Christ. I'm not doing that again.'

'What exactly?' said Munro, taking the pack from her back.

'A retreat. Nothing but bloody carrots and cabbage for a week, and no alcohol. Remind me, if I ever feel the need to reach my inner self again, I'll use a coat hanger. I feel like death.'

'Good! Tell me, lassie, have you any plans. Right now, I mean?'

'Yes,' said West. 'Large vodka, train, plane, home. In that order. Then, it's back to work.'

'So, you've not left the force then?'

'Couldn't decide. I thought the break would do me good, help me focus, get some bloody direction in my life.'

'And has it?' said Munro.

'Has it fuck. Anyway, why are you so interested? Why are you here?'

'A fortuitous coincidence. I thought you might like to … lend me a hand.'

'Lend you a hand?' said West, suspiciously. 'What are you doing, decorating?'

'No, no, I've taken on a wee case, that's all, nothing big, won't take long.'

'Impossible,' said West, 'besides, I can't work up here, not without…'

'Och, a minor point, Charlie,' said Munro, 'don't you worry about that, it's all sorted.'

West reached for her rucksack and shook her head.

'Sorry, James, look, I'm not being funny, it's been nice

seeing you and all, but I've just got off the ferry, I'm tired and I'm hungry, besides, I've no clothes or…'

'You've a bag full of clothes, what more do you need?' said Munro. 'Just a few days, think of it as an extended holiday.'

'No.'

'Okay,' said Munro, opening the car door, 'well, at least I tried. Have a good trip, Charlie, as you say, it was nice to catch up, you take care of yourself, you hear.'

'I, er, I don't suppose you're heading towards the airport, are you?' said West.

'No, opposite direction, I'm afraid. I'm away for my lunch, just now.'

'Lunch?'

'Aye. It's on expenses, too. I was thinking a large steak and a glass or two of red.'

'Christ, you know how to take advantage, don't you?'

Chapter 4

Crawford, an advocate of punctuality, checked her watch and huffed impatiently as Doctor Clark, bored with the silence, wriggled uneasily in his seat.

'You'll forgive my tardiness,' said McGreevy, as he and Campbell breezed through the door, 'the Sergeant here had to queue, folk are awful hungry this time of day.'

'Well, as you come bearing gifts,' said Crawford, 'consider yourself forgiven. What have you got?'

'Coffee, croissants, chocolate doughnuts, oh, and some plain toast for the Doctor, should you be fretting about your cholesterol and the like.'

Clark smiled and reached for a doughnut.

'That,' he said, with a sarcastic grin, 'is the least of my problems.'

'Good. Let's get down to it,' said Crawford. 'Doctor Clark, I trust the post-mortem confirmed your suspicions?'

'Right enough,' said Clark, brushing crumbs from his report, 'so, here's the thing. First of all, as I suspected, the blow to the head didnae come from a fall. The wound is perfectly round and the trauma around the area of impact suggests she was struck from behind with a small, flat-faced instrument, my guess is, a hammer of sorts.'

'Does that... I mean, is that what killed her?' said Campbell.

'No. It would have given her a nasty headache and knocked her over, no doubt about that, but not enough to kill her. One thing's for sure, once she was down, she wasnae capable of getting up again.'

'And that would be, why?' said Crawford.

'Intoxication.'

'You mean she was blootered?' said Campbell.

'Aye, but that's not all. See, we found oxalate crystals in the kidneys, which is, to say the least, unusual; it causes renal failure, so we sent bloods to toxicology which not only confirmed the high level of alcohol...'

'Is *that* what killed her?' said McGreevy.

'Not quite. We also found glycolic acid, acetone, and formic acid.'

'Doctor Clark,' said Crawford, raising her eyebrows, 'unless those are the ingredients of a particularly powerful cocktail, and you know where I can get one, you'd best elucidate.'

'Okay. Glycolic acid increases the pH of the blood which leads to hyperventilation as the body tries to rid itself of excess carbon dioxide. Acetone depresses the activity of the nervous system, so basically you'd lose control of your senses. Literally. And the formic acid would explain why her pupils were constricted, it damages the optic nerve.'

'So, how did all of that get into her body?' said McGreevy, perplexed.

'Easy,' said Clark. 'She was poisoned. Ethylene glycol. Anti-freeze to you and me.'

'Anti-freeze? But surely,' said Campbell, 'does it not taste...?'

'That's the beauty of it,' said Clark, 'mixed with alcohol, it's virtually undetectable. No taste, no odour.'

'So, that's what killed her?' said Crawford, sipping her coffee. 'You're saying she was deliberately poisoned?'

19

'Aye. And it's not pleasant, either. See, it's slow-acting, has to work its way around the body. She'd have experienced some nausea and dizziness to start with, then her eyesight would have failed before losing control of her bowels. It's a fearful position to be in, I mean, can you imagine the mental trauma of not knowing what was happening to your body? The stress on the heart would have been enormous.'

'Could we have done anything to save her?' said Campbell. 'If we'd got there sooner, maybe?'

'No, Sergeant, I'm afraid not, see, once ingested, unless you do something within the hour, you've had it.'

'Well,' said Crawford, downing her cup, 'I can think of better of ways to start the day, but needs must. So, final question, do we know who she is?'

'No,' said Clark.

'But she was carrying a couple of bank cards,' said Campbell, 'so at least we have a name to go on.'

'Good,' said Crawford, in that case, I'll inform CID. Gentlemen.'

McGreevy gently closed the door behind Clark and Campbell as they left the room.

'Isobel,' he said, 'a wee word, if I may.'

'Of course Nick, what's up?'

'CID. You know…'

'I know; you don't exactly see eye to eye…'

'Can you blame me?' said McGreevy, 'After last time?'

'I admit, they can be a bit, boisterous…'

'Boisterous? That's an understatement.'

'But there's nothing I can do about it. It's a murder, they're detectives, that's how it works.'

'I know Isobel, but just hear me out. Five days. That's all I'm asking. Give me five days to look into this, and if I don't get anywhere, fair enough, give it to Greenock.'

'Am I missing something, Nick?' said Crawford, with an inquisitive tilt of the head. 'Are you a D.I. now?'

'No, but, I… I know a man who is. Used to be.'

'And that would be?'

'James. James…'

'Munro?' said Crawford, mildly surprised.

'Aye. James Munro.'

'I thought he'd moved south.'

'He did. And now he's back.'

'But he's retired, is he not?'

'Aye, he is, but… we could, you know…'

Crawford sat down, her brow furrowed as though stuck on a 13 across.

'This is highly unconventional Nick,' she said, 'I'm not sure I can…'

'Och, Isobel, come on, five days. I need someone on my patch who knows the meaning of the word *discreet*, someone who can make enquiries without ruffling feathers.'

'If the senior Fiscal finds out, I could be…'

'Five days.'

Crawford stared blankly into space, contemplating the consequences.

'Okay,' she said, reluctantly, 'okay. Five days Nick. And no-one's to know. No-one but your office. Understand? And I want daily updates. Oh, and I'd better have a word with Munro, too.'

'Isobel, you're a doll. Leave it to us.'

* * *

As a young officer, Constable Reid could not be faulted for his drive and determination, intent, as he was, on joining the drugs squad where a helmet wouldn't play havoc with his carefully coiffed hair, nor a uniform hinder his appearance. By way of gaining as much inside knowledge as possible into the workings of the underworld, he had his nose buried in a copy of *Mr. Nice* when his superiors returned.

'Duncan,' said McGreevy, tossing his cap on the desk.

'Chief. Sergeant.'

'All good?'

'Aye,' said Reid, 'just a burglar alarm on Bute Street. Jamie, I mean Constable Shaw's seeing to it now. Oh, and you've a couple of visitors…'

'Visitors?' said McGreevy. 'It's not my birthday, who would…'

'A gentleman and a young lady. Thing is, chief, the girl, she looks a bit, well, down on her luck, so I made them both a brew and sat them in your office, hope that's okay, we've not enough chairs out here.'

'Fine, Duncan, fine. I don't suppose you managed to get a name, by any chance?'

'Oh, aye, sorry chief, said his name's Munro.'

McGreevy turned to Campbell, smiled broadly and slapped him on the back.

'Maybe it's my birthday after all,' he said. 'Come with me, Iain, there's someone you need to meet.'

McGreevy opened the door to find Munro, as usual in a military stance, legs akimbo, hands clasped behind his back, reading a poster on the wall, while slumped in a chair, half-asleep, sat a young, damp-haired lady, her head lolled to one side, looking to all intents and purposes as if she'd expired.

'James!' he said. 'You made it. I cannae tell you how glad I am to see you.'

He flicked and his head in the direction of West.

'And this would be…'

'Detective Sergeant Charlotte West,' said Munro. 'City of London Police. Charlie!'

West woke with a start and stood, slightly befuddled.

'Sorry, must have…'

'City of London? My, my, we are privileged,' said McGreevy. 'Pleased to meet you, I'm Inspector McGreevy and this is Sergeant Iain Campbell.'

'Good,' said Munro, 'well, now that we're all acquainted, perhaps we could…'

'Aye, take a seat,' said McGreevy. 'We're just back from the Fiscal's office, and we've got the pathologist's report, so…'

'No, no, no,' said Munro, shaking his head. 'Nick, the lassie's just off the boat, I've driven for two hours to get here, she needs to freshen up and we both need to get some food in our bellies, so, if it's all the same with you…'

'Of course,' said McGreevy. 'The Kip Hotel, I'll get Duncan to show you where it is. See you back here in say, an hour?'

'Aye,' said Munro, 'maybe two.'

* * *

Constable Reid, relishing his role as escort and the opportunity to patrol the mean streets of Inverkip like some maverick cop on the prowl, led Munro to the hotel, gave a blast on the siren and flashed his hazards before speeding away. West sat back, turned to Munro and heaved a sigh.

'How the hell did I end up here?' she said. 'A couple of hours ago, I was on my way home.'

Munro smiled.

'Fate,' he said. 'So, tell me Charlie, how are you, really?'

'I'm okay. I think. I'm okay.'

'Good. And did you learn anything from your time on the… retreat?'

'I did,' said West, nodding. 'I did. I learned that I don't like singing or chanting. And I don't like silence. And I don't like sushi, never have, never will. I like my steak and I like a drink, and I'm not going to take any shit anymore. From anyone. You know what? I'm good at what I do, James, damned good, but… you knew that anyway.'

* * *

Campbell, taken aback, stood and smiled, slightly embarrassed as West, followed by Munro, entered the office.

'Sergeant West,' he said, 'you look, I mean, you look…'

'Amazing?'

'Aye, amazing, I mean…'

'Thank you,' said West, 'I scrub up well when I have to, and by the way, the name's Charlie.'

'Sergeant Campbell,' said McGreevy, grinning, 'when you've stopped drooling, perhaps you could ask Duncan to join us, I'm sure he'll prove an invaluable asset to the team. How's the hotel, James? Comfortable enough?'

'Oh, aye, nice, wee restaurant, too.'

'Pity we didn't make use of it,' said West.

'I've taken the liberty of setting up a tab,' said Munro, 'you can sort it when we leave.'

'Okay,' said McGreevy, 'just go easy on the bar, James, eh? So, Iain, as you were first on the scene, perhaps you'd like to fill us all in, from the top.'

'Chief. I'll keep it brief, there's a full report from the pathologist here, you can read through it later. So, we have a female, as yet unidentified, about mid-fifties, found in Daff Glen, face down in the burn…'

'Burn?' said West, frowning.

'It's a river, Charlie,' said Campbell, 'a small river.'

'Okay.'

'She's a wound to the back of the head, hit with a blunt instrument, but here's the thing, that's not what killed her, she was poisoned, anti-freeze. Also, there were high levels of alcohol in the blood. The only clue we have as to her identity are these two bank cards, that's all she was carrying.'

Campbell slid them across the table.

'Have these been dusted?' said West.

'Er, no, no,' said Campbell, 'I'm afraid by the time we'd hauled her from the water and the medics, you know…'

'Raiffeisen Bank?' said West, 'Where's that?'

'Germany,' said McGreevy, 'I mean, I'm guessing, but it sounds German.'

Munro picked up a card and studied it carefully.

'Doris Day,' he said.

'Sorry Nick, you've lost me,' said McGreevy.

'Kappelhoff. That was Doris Day's real name.'

'Doris who?' said Reid. 'Who's Doris...'

'Och, Duncan, Doris Day man! Calamity Jane, Que Sera Sera, never mind. Okay, Nick, Iain, Duncan, there cannae be that many Kappelhoffs in the area, let alone the whole of Scotland, run a check and see...'

'There is another,' said Constable Reid.

'What?' said McGreevy.

'The shoe man, you know, Rudy, his name's Kappelhoff.'

'I thought it was Ruben.'

'It is. Ruben Kappelhoff.'

'Excellent,' said Munro, 'see, we're off to a flying start already. Charlie, we'll pay him a visit later, now, has anyone checked these cards? Have you called the Raiffeisen Bank?'

'No, not yet,' said Campbell, 'see, those cards, they're out of date, 14 years old, I mean, what use would they be to...?'

'She was carrying them for a reason, Iain. Duncan, you call the bank, get any information you can on this Freida Kappelhoff, last known address, when the account was closed, that sort of thing.'

'Roger that, chief.'

'We should put out an appeal, too,' said McGreevy.

'An appeal?' said Munro.

'Aye, you know, missing person, that sort of thing.'

'She's not missing, Nick, we've found her. However, perhaps you'd like to advertise the fact we have an unidentified body on our hands and so put the fear of God into the public domain?'

'Well, no, not quite, I mean...'

'No appeal,' said Munro, 'no tv, no press. Not until we know who she is, not until we have a name, is that clear?'

'Aye, okay, you know best.'

'What about her clothes? Are they at the hospital?'

'No,' said Campbell, 'I have them here, all bagged and sealed.'

'Good. We'll take a look later, now, Iain, I need you to show us where you found her.'

'Oh, James,' said McGreevy, as they stood to leave, 'one thing, when you get back, we should go see Isobel.'

'Aye, okay. Who's Isobel?'

'The Fiscal.'

Chapter 5

Sergeant West shielded her eyes from the low, afternoon sun, stood stock-still and, underwhelmed by her surroundings, turned her nose up at the smell of damp, decaying leaves, as the Daff, its waters still high, surged hurriedly by.

'It's beautiful here,' said Munro quietly, 'so, beautiful.'

'It's a dank, boggy wood with a river, James. Get over it.'

'Nothing like a city girl to lend a new perspective on things,' quipped Campbell. 'Here, this is where I found her.'

'Okay,' said Munro, 'and this fellow with the dog, where was he?'

'Where she should have been, over there, on the opposite bank, there's a footpath along the top.'

'And you think this is where she tried to cross?'

'Definitely,' said Campbell. 'It's only knee deep here, if you know where to tread.'

'And where did you search?'

'Hereabouts.'

'Then you've been looking in the wrong place,' said Munro. 'We need to be over there. Charlie, best take off your boots.'

'Are you mad?' said West, scowling.

'It's alright, Charlie,' said Campbell, laughing, 'there's a ford up the way, here. Follow me.'

Munro looked across the burn to where Freida Kappelhoff had lain, turned around and studied the embankment up to the path. A trail, subtle and unintentional, had been cleared through the sparse undergrowth, as though someone, or something, had fallen down the slope. Fallen twigs snapped underfoot as he signalled to the others to follow and made his way to the top, scouring the ground for clues at a painstakingly slow pace.

'Was Freida a smoker?' he said, as he reached the path, squatted on his haunches and retrieved a cigarette butt from the ground.

'No idea, chief,' said Campbell, 'but I can ask the doctor, why?'

'See here, these are German, 'HB'. I don't partake myself, but even I know these are not, what you might call, a popular brand.'

'But anyone could've tossed those there,' said West.

'Right enough, Charlie,' said Munro, 'anyone who was here long enough to smoke three of them. Bag this, and there's two more, just there. Whoever was here, was lingering. Iain, where will this take us, if we follow the path?'

'The village, chief, Main Street; that's where you'll find Rudy, and your hotel.'

'Okay, listen, light's fading, I need this area searched tomorrow, 100-yard radius from here, you never know, we may find something. Charlie, let's you and I go see this Ruben fellow, and keep your eyes peeled.'

* * *

Munro and West stood side by side and eyed the neglected bungalow of a building, its peeling paintwork, weathered sign and filthy windows overshadowed by the

28

surrounding rows of pebble-dashed terraces.

'Not the kind of place I'd trust with my Jimmys,' said West, facetiously.

'Your what?' said Munro, as they approached the shop.

West smiled.

'Never mind, grandad,' she said, 'looks like he's gone home, shall we come back tomorrow?'

Munro peered inside.

'There's a light,' he said, squinting through the glass, 'in the back room, there.'

He knocked the door, hard. A stocky figure in a sweatshirt with a towel draped around his neck, entered the shop, glowered at them and, with a dismissive wave of the arm, shouted something unintelligible. Munro held a hand to his ear, feigning deafness.

'Closed!' yelled Kappelhoff, as he yanked open the front door. 'Go away, bring your shoes tomorrow, I... wait, where are your shoes? What are you wanting?'

West smiled politely.

'This is Detective Inspector Munro,' she said, 'and I'm D.S. West. Can we have a...'

'What? You are police?' said Kappelhoff. 'You come to my work, my home, at this hour, disturbing me? I am honest, hard-working man, why do you harass me? You like Stasi, always picking on the small man, easy prey for you blood-thirsty, fascist pigs.'

'Well, we have to do something to fill our time,' said Munro, softly, 'all the same, we'd like a wee word, please; unless, of course, you'd rather be arrested for disturbing the peace?'

'Disturb? I not...'

'Threatening behaviour too.'

Kappelhoff stood aside and ushered them into the back room which, with it's white-tiled floor, Formica-topped table and galvanised sink, looked more like a hospital kitchen from the 1950s than a lounge. A single, leather armchair sat in the corner, beside it, a small table piled high with unopened mail and a radio tuned to an overseas station. He switched it off.

'Thank you,' said Munro, surveying his surroundings. 'Now, we're not here to persecute you, Mr. Kappelhoff, we'd just like to ask you a few questions…'

'Always questions! I pay my taxes; I don't make trouble…'

'About Freida.'

Kappelhoff look stunned.

'Freida?' he whispered.

'Aye. I'm assuming Freida is your wife?'

'Yes, yes, but Freida and I, we divorce, long time ago. I have not seen her in many years. What has happened?'

'We've, er, we've found a body,' said West, 'and we think it might be her.'

Kappelhoff placed a hand on the table to steady himself and slowly sat.

'A body?' he whispered.

'I'm afraid so,' said Munro. 'Sorry, it must be a shock, would you like a moment to…?'

'No, no. I am alright. Where did you find this body?'

'Daff Glen,' said West, 'in the burn, it looks like she was… it looks like she may have drowned.'

'And you are sure it is Freida?' said Kappelhoff.

'Well, no,' said Munro, 'that's why we're here, we need your help.'

'The police, wanting help from a poor immigrant? I should tell the papers, this is news.'

Munro lowered his head and smiled.

'Okay, see here, Mr. Kappelhoff,' he said, 'the only way we'll know if it is Freida, is if we can make a positive I.D. of the body and, as you were her husband, I think you're the man for the job. Are you up for it?'

'Of course, but, God-willing, it is not.'

'Good. We can pick you up. Tomorrow morning. Would 9 o'clock be okay?'

'Yes, yes, 9 o'clock will be…'

Munro unzipped his jacket and sat down.

'Listen,' he said, 'I know this might be difficult but there's a couple of questions I need to ask.'

Kappelhoff glanced at West and nodded.

'Do you smoke?' said Munro.

'Smoke? No.'

'How about Freida?'

'No, at least not when she was my wife.'

'Okay, good. Now, do you have a bank account, in Germany? With the Raiffeisen Bank?'

'No,' said Kappelhoff, 'my monies are here, with Clydesdale Bank.'

'You're quite sure?' said Munro. 'Because we found a bank card with your wife's name on it, Freida Kappelhoff.'

'Oh, yes, Freida, she had monies with Raiffeisen Bank, since before we met, but that is her monies, Freida was wealthy lady back in Schleswig, but her name is Brandt, Freida Brandt. Why should she use my name when we not married?'

'Perhaps she forgot to change it after the divorce?' said West.

Kappelhoff grinned menacingly at West.

'If you want to forget the past, lady,' he said, 'the first thing you do is reclaim your name.'

'Just one last question then, Mr. Kappelhoff,' said Munro, 'you don't have to answer if you don't want to, but, why did you and Freida divorce?'

Kappelhoff hung his head and smiled wistfully.

'I did not want divorce but she grew tired of the humble shoemaker she once loved, I was, too poor for her… tastes.'

'I see,' said Munro, 'and was it, amicable? I mean, did you and Freida part on friendly terms?'

Kappelhoff slammed his fist on the table.

'No!' he said, 'I was mad, of course, I was mad! I knew she was seeing another man but I didn't care, she was my Freida. Then she says to me one day she is going, she has found another man, an educated man with more monies, just like that! Then she leaves. I could have slit her throat!'

'Have you ever heard of anger management?' said West, sarcastically.

'What?'

'Ignore her,' said Munro, 'tell me, do you know who this man was?'

'Lucky for him, I did not.'

* * *

'Chief!' said Duncan, rather too enthusiastically for Munro's liking, as they returned to the station.

'Duncan, have you ever heard of Diazepam?' he said.

'No, chief, should I…'

'It's been a long day, laddie, now, take a deep breath and hold it while Charlie and I remove our coats, sit down, and wait for you to bring us our tea.'

'Chief.'

McGreevy sauntered in from his office.

'James,' he said, 'I know it's getting late but don't forget we've yet to see Isobel.'

'Aye, okay Nick, all in good time.'

'How'd you get on with Rudy?' said McGreevy.

'He's what you might call… volatile. Aye, that's the word, I think, volatile.'

'Obviously has issues,' said West, 'a week on the Holy Isle would put him straight.'

McGreevy smiled as Constable Reid returned with two mugs of tea.

'Duncan here, has some interesting news for you,' he said.

'You don't say?' said Munro. 'Okay, Duncan, take a seat, oh, before I forget, listen, assuming you've still no address for Freida, try Brandt – that was her maiden name.'

'Roger that, chief, but there's no need.'

'You have been busy,' said West.

'Miss. So, Raiffeisen Bank,' said Reid, grinning.

'Yes?'

'The bank cards.'

'Yes?'

'Well, they're two separate accounts, one is a current account and the other, savings, and both accounts are… active.'

'Is that so?' said Munro, grimacing as he sipped his sugarless brew.

'Every month, the equivalent of £2,500 is transferred from the savings account to the current.'

'£2,500?' said Munro. 'My, my, this Freida must be a millionaire.'

'She is,' said Reid, 'in euros, anyway. The current balance is 1,180,000, that's about £920,000.'

'I see,' said Munro.

'And that's not all. After the monthly transfer, there's a flurry of activity on the account, cash withdrawals, maximum amount, till it's all gone.'

'Do we know where?'

'All over the place, chief. Greenock, Paisley, Glasgow, Falkirk, Ayr.'

'Is that it?'

'Not quite. All the statements and replacement cards are sent to an address in Skelmorlie.'

'And, of course you've checked that that is the last known address for Freida?'

'Well, no, not exactly; I mean, not yet, chief. That's next on my…'

'Don't worry, Duncan,' said Munro, smiling, 'we'll take a wee look tomorrow. Listen, well done laddie. Good work. Now, Charlie, I think you've earned yourself a wee drink, take yourself off to the hotel, I'll be along as soon as I've seen the Fiscal.'

West stood abruptly and grabbed her coat.

'That's the best idea you've had all day,' she said, 'hold

on, how do I get there? Is it walkable?'

Sergeant Campbell cleared his throat with a subtle cough.

'I could, er, I could run you there, Charlie,' he said. 'It's not far.'

'Are you sure?' said West. 'Don't you have work to do?'

'No, no, I'm finished now, anyway.'

'Very kind, Iain, thanks. Hope your wife doesn't get jealous.'

'Wife? Oh, I'm not married, Charlie, I'm as single as they come.'

* * *

Crawford, Scotch in hand, stared at the screen, her patience waning with every pop-up ad or invitation to take part in a survey that interrupted her quest for a decent Margaux. A knock on the door saved her from screaming aloud. McGreevy entered before she could answer, followed by Munro. She regarded his battle-weary features with intrigue, taken aback by the alluring glare of his steely, blue-eyed gaze.

'James Munro,' she said, proffering her hand as she stood.

'Aye,' he said, 'that's me.'

Munro was struck by her somewhat sophisticated appearance, the dark, brown hair cut neatly to a bob, the fringe dusting the top of her eyebrows, the pearl stud earrings, the delicate, silver chain around her neck and the absence of a ring on her left hand. The corner of his mouth rose impulsively.

'And you must be Isobel.'

'Drink?' she said.

'Thank you, no. I'll not stay long,' said Munro.

'Very well,' said Crawford. 'You've obviously got a lot on your plate, so I'll be brief. I'm sticking my neck out here, James. If anyone finds out I've agreed to let a retired police officer look into this case, especially the senior

Fiscal, I'll be for the chop. Five days, understood? Not a minute more.'

Munro said nothing, his face expressionless.

'And keep your head down,' she continued, 'act like a tourist, or … or something.'

'Nae bother,' said Munro, 'you'll not even know I'm here.'

Crawford smiled.

'Good. Now, are you sure you won't…?'

'No. Thanks all the same. There's somewhere I have to be.'

Crawford returned to her seat and took a sip of whisky as the door closed behind him.

'Christ, he's a hard bastard, isn't he?' she said, quietly.

'Has to be,' said McGreevy. 'Wouldn't have a reputation if he wasn't.'

'Even so,' said Crawford, 'there's something, dangerously attractive about him, something reckless.'

'You've no chance,' said McGreevy, grinning, 'that's a man who loves his wife.'

'Wife? But I thought she died? In that terrible fire?'

'Aye, she did that, Isobel. She did that.'

* * *

Munro was not unsociable by nature, as long as the company he kept was of his own choosing, he could hold court as well as the next man, but a crowded inn, rammed with folk, shoulder to shoulder, clearly already on their fourth or fifth round of drinks and shouting rather than talking, was something he found difficult to tolerate. He spied a couple at the bar, perched on stools, sharing a joke and struggling to make themselves heard above the din.

'Iain,' he said, 'I didn't expect to see you here.'

Sergeant Campbell, taken off guard, stood and looked at Munro with an air of unease, as though he'd been caught in the throes of a clandestine affair with his daughter.

'Chief,' he said, draining his glass, 'just a, just a wee

snifter after work, you know.'

'I do indeed, Iain. I do indeed.'

'Just thought I'd sit with Charlie, till you got here, so she didn't… get bored.'

'That's very kind of you Iain,' said Munro, 'very kind, indeed. Let me reward your chivalry with a wee drink.'

'Oh, no, thanks chief, I think I better…'

'Will you not stay for supper, then? I hear they've a fine menu, here.'

'Oh, they have, you'll not be disappointed, but I should… go.'

'Spoilsport,' said West, as they watched Campbell fight his way to the door, 'he's quite sweet really. Funny too.'

Munro gave her a wink.

'We'd best order those steaks, lassie,' he said, grinning, 'if you've your eye on a Scotsman, you'll need to keep your strength up.'

Chapter 6

Kappelhoff counted the bank of stainless steel doors, four rows of eight, 32 in total, and turned to Clark bewildered, as the bright, fluorescent strip lights fizzled overhead.

'There are people,' he said, his voice barely more than a whisper, 'in all these boxes?'

'Fortunately not,' said Clark as he opened number 19, 'it's okay, there's nothing to worry about.'

'Ready?' said Munro.

Kappelhoff took a deep breath.

'Ready.'

West turned away as Clark pulled back the sheet.

'She looks ... she looks so ... peaceful,' said Kappelhoff.

'Is it Freida?' said Munro.

Kappelhoff stared at the cadaver, entranced, and paused before answering.

'Well, it looks like her,' he said, 'but...'

'But what?' said Munro.

'I can't be sure, I mean, it's many years since we, twenty years, she looks so much ... older, so many lines on her face, I'm not...'

'It's alright, Rudy,' said West, 'don't say unless you're

absolutely certain.'

'I am sorry. I am not, almost, but…'

'No problem,' said West, 'but listen, there's something that might help, did Freida have any identifying marks, like a scar, or a mole or a birthmark? Anything like that?'

Kappelhoff, still staring at the body, shook his head.

'No,' he said, 'that, I would remember.'

'How about family?' said Munro. 'Did Freida have any brothers or sisters?'

'A sister. She has a sister. Mathild.'

'Did you keep in touch?'

'No, they weren't close, and after the divorce, why would I…?'

'Fair enough Mr. Kappelhoff,' said Munro as Clark slid the body home and closed the door, 'fair enough. Come on, we'll take you back, just one last thing before we go, we need a DNA sample.'

'A what?'

'DNA. It's perfectly harmless, we just need to take a swab from the inside of your cheek, takes two seconds.'

'Inside my cheek? What else? A pound of flesh, maybe? You think I am guilty? You think I would do such a thing?'

'No, no, nothing like that. It will simply assist us with our inquiry, that's all.'

Kappelhoff sighed and raised his hands in surrender.

'Alright, alright,' he said, 'you want my fingerprints, too? Maybe you should also take a picture.'

Doctor Clark collared Munro as West escorted Kappelhoff back to the car.

'A quick word, Inspector,' he said, 'Sergeant Campbell asked me to check if this lady was a smoker, is that right?'

'Oh, aye, Doctor, we found a cigarette or two at the scene, may be nothing, but…'

'Well, I'm glad to say, she wasn't, not even a nicotine stain on her fingers. In fact, considering her age, she was in rude health. Were it not for her untimely demise, I'd say she had another twenty years in her, at least.'

* * *

'Morning, Iain,' said West, smiling coyly as they returned to the station.

'Charlie, chief.'

'And how was your evening, Iain?' said Munro.

'I've had better,' said Campbell, casting a sly glance at West, 'I mean, quiet. Quiet night, chief.'

'Good. Is Nick hereabouts, or is he…?'

'Here, James,' said McGreevy, stepping in from his office, 'how was it? Did Rudy give you a positive ID?'

'No, he did not, he says it's been too long since he saw her last, and I cannae blame the fellow, I can barely remember who was in the bar last night.'

Campbell squirmed in his seat.

'So, what do we do now?' said McGreevy. 'About IDing the body?'

'We have Freida's DNA, Nick,' said Munro, 'so we'll try and trace her next of kin. Duncan, I think this is something you'll enjoy. Duncan!'

Constable Reid, leaning on the front desk, closed his book and turned to face Munro.

'Sorry, chief, just getting to a good bit.'

'Well, I've an even better bit here. Listen, I need you to find a relative of Freida's, she's a sister, name of Mathild, maiden name, Brandt.'

'Roger that, chief.'

'Start in Schleswig.'

'Schleswig?' said Reid, looking perplexed.

'Schleswig-Holstein, it's a province in Germany, that's where she's from.'

Munro looked frantically around the office, as though he'd lost something incredibly precious. His eyes settled on West.

'If Duncan's looking for Freida's relative,' he said, 'who on earth is going to make the tea?'

West smiled and made for the kitchen as Munro hung

his coat on the back of a chair and took a seat opposite Sergeant Campbell.

'So, Iain,' he said, 'your turn. How's the search going? Have you some lads up there, just now?'

'No chief,' said Campbell, leaning back and folding his arms, 'all done.'

'All done? Already?'

'Aye, we were there first light. Most of the undergrowth was too thick to get through but we did cover pretty much the whole area, as you asked. If we'd had more men, we could've done a more thorough search, but…'

'So, that's it?' sighed Munro. 'I don't suppose you found anything, did you?'

'No,' said Campbell, reaching beneath his desk, 'just this,'

He held up a clear, plastic bag containing a small hammer, wooden shaft, approximately 12" long, with a polished head.

'Not the kind of thing you'd lose in the middle of the glen, now, is it?'

Munro glanced at Campbell, smiled appreciatively and took the bag.

'It's awfully clean,' he said. 'You've not wiped this, have you?'

'No, chief. Gloves, bagged and sealed.'

'Where was it?'

'About twenty yards from the path.'

'Good. Then it's not lain there long; this was tossed there recently.'

'Aye,' said Campbell, 'one other thing, I took the liberty of measuring the diameter of face, about an inch and a quarter, same size as the wound to the back of Freida's head.'

Munro sat back and grinned.

'You know something, Iain,' he said, 'keep this up and you'll make detective in no time. Lab, please, we need prints, and see if they can lift a sample off the head, something that matches Freida's DNA.'

West returned with two mugs of tea and took Campbell's vacant seat.

'Thanks, Charlie,' said Munro, 'next task, start going through Freida's clothes, see if you can find anything that shouldn't be there.'

'No probs,' she said. 'So, what do you make of the hammer? Think that's our weapon?'

'Aye, looks like it, I reckon our Freida was struck on the path, just where we found the cigarettes, before stumbling down the bank and into the burn. And I reckon it was someone she knew. I'd say they were there a wee while, chatting, or arguing. And whoever attacked her, was fond of foreign … Duncan!'

Constable Reid, annoyed at the interruption in his pursuit of Frau Brandt, raised his head and frowned.

'Chief?'

'Duncan, drop that for a wee second,' said Munro, 'get hold of every hotel, B&B and guest house in the area and see if they've anyone staying with them from Germany, in particular, anyone travelling alone.'

'Roger that, chief! Oh, hello Mrs. Fraser, what brings you here?'

A short, bespectacled woman, mature in years, walked tentatively towards the front desk and smiled nervously.

'Hello, Duncan,' she said timidly, embarrassed that she may be taking him away from his work, 'I wonder if I can have a wee word.'

'Of course, you can, Mrs. Fraser, how can I help?'

'Well, as you know, I'm not one to make a fuss but, I'm a wee bit, concerned.'

'What about?' said Reid.

'My friend, we work together and she's still not come. She's usually very punctual.'

'And is this just this morning, Mrs. F? Maybe she's been delayed.'

'No,' said Fraser, reaching for a tissue, 'it's three days now. I do hope nothing's happened to her.'

'Okay, tell you what, why don't we start with her name, then we'll take it from there.'

'Thank you, Duncan. It's Freida, Freida…'

Munro spun around and leapt from his chair.

'Excuse me,' he said as he approached the desk, scowling, 'did I hear correctly? Did you say Freida?'

Fraser, startled by his less than subtle approach, instinctively took a step back and drew her bag to her chest.

'Aye, that's right. Freida Kappelhoff,' she said anxiously. 'And who are you? Duncan, should I be talking to this…'

'It's okay, this is Detective Inspector Munro. Chief, this is Mrs. Fraser, friend of the family, so to speak. She works up at the big house.'

Munro gave her a warm smile and walked around the counter to greet her properly.

'Sorry,' he said, 'I didnae mean to alarm you. The big house, you say? What's that?'

'The manor, chief, up on the estate. Mrs. Fraser's a cracking cook.'

'Och, Duncan, stop it now, I am not. I just cook, that's all.'

'Well,' said Munro, extending an arm, 'why not come round and sit with us and I'll take some details. Would you care for a drink? A cup of tea maybe?'

'No, no,' she said, taking a seat.

'This is Detective Sergeant West, now what's all this about your friend, Freida?'

'Well,' said Fraser, taking a deep breath, 'she's a lovely lady, ever so nice, and she likes her routine, punctual to the second, you could set your watch by her.'

'So, you work together?' said West.

'Aye, in the kitchens. Well, it was Friday evening, we'd finished work and she said she was going into town…'

'Inverkip?'

'That's right, Inverkip, for a wee drink, with a gentleman friend of hers. To be honest, I was a little surprised.'

'And why was that?'

'She wasn't feeling herself, she looked a little … peaky. We'd had a few glasses of wine the night before, you see. We often do that, drink and a wee chit chat. Have to say, I didn't feel that great myself.'

'And where was that? Did you go out?'

'Oh, no, we don't do that. It was at Freida's place. We take it in turns, you see.'

'Okay, so, she went out, you say?'

'Aye, she insisted on going, said her friend had gone to the trouble of booking a table somewhere, so she couldnae let him down.'

'Go on,' said Munro.

'Well, Saturday's her day off, so when she didn't come back, I thought nothing of it, I just assumed she was having some fun. But she's still not back.'

'Have you been to see her?' said West. 'Tried knocking the door, see if she's…'

'We stay at the house,' said Fraser, 'live-in, her rooms are next to mine. We don't get paid much but we get free accommodation, and food, of course.'

'I see,' said Munro, 'and would you happen to know who this gentleman friend is? The one she went to meet?'

Fraser fell silent and fiddled with the strap on her bag, rankled by the question.

'Is there something wrong?' said West.

'Let's just say, I have an idea,' said Fraser, 'but that's all it is, an idea.'

'Okay, but you'll not say who?' said Munro.

'No. The man has a family. It wouldn't be right to jeopardise his marriage. I couldn't do that.'

'Fair enough, Mrs. Fraser. Fair enough.'

'Tell me,' said West, 'how long have you two known

each other?'

'Oh, long enough, we're like sisters, really. Must be all of twelve years, or thereabouts.'

'Just to be sure, now,' said Munro, 'could you give us a wee description of your friend.'

Fraser raised her eyes to the ceiling and frowned.

'Taller than me,' she said, 'not by much, but taller, all the same. Not a big lass, slight, you might say, mousey hair, and pretty – very attractive for her age.'

Munro stood, clasped his hands behind his back and strode around the table before returning to his seat.

'Mrs. Fraser,' he said with a sigh, folding his hands beneath his chin, 'I'm afraid I've some bad news. See, we've found a body, and it appears to match the description of your friend.'

Fraser said nothing. Stunned, she stared at Munro, held his gaze for a few seconds, then turned her attention to West, half expecting her to utter something to the contrary.

'What?' she whispered, 'I mean, where, where did you find her? What happened?'

'In the burn, it looks as though she drowned,' said Munro, fearful of upsetting her further.

'I see,' said Fraser, quietly, shaking her head. 'I see.'

'Listen,' said West, softly, 'I know you must be in shock, but the thing is, we have no way of positively identifying the body and, as you were obviously close friends, and quite possibly one the last people to see her alive, I wonder, would you mind…'

'You want me to come to the mortuary? And look at the body? And tell you if it's her?'

'Only if you're up to it.'

Fraser closed her eyes and nodded.

'It's the least I can do,' she said. 'When should we…'

'Whenever you're ready,' said Munro, 'it's entirely up to you. Tomorrow…'

'Will we go now? I've an hour before my shift, I think

44

I'd like to get it…'

'Of course,' said Munro, 'I'll run you there myself, and once we're done, I'll drop you back at the house. You'll have to show me the way, mind.'

'Och, there's no need, Inspector, I've my car outside.'

Chapter 7

'There y'are, Charlie,' said Sergeant Campbell as he smoothed a white, polythene dust sheet over the desk, 'best we can do.'

He stood back and watched, transfixed, as West laid out Freida's waxed cotton jacket and inspected it closely with a magnifying glass.

'So, this is what detectives do all day, is it?' he said, quietly.

'Mostly,' said West, 'when we're not down the pub or fitting-up narks. Freida had dark blonde hair, right Iain?'

'Aye Charlie, dark blonde, that's right.'

'Then who belongs to these?' she said, gently retrieving two red hairs snagged around a button on the cuff with a pair of tweezers. 'Bag, please.'

A few specks of dried mud fell from a rip along the left shoulder seam as she flipped the jacket over.

'So, narks aside,' said Campbell, 'you're not averse to a trip down the pub now and then?'

'Only weekdays and weekends,' said West as she reached for a torch, 'I'm trying to cut down. Lights please.'

'Sorry?'

'Lights. Out.'

Campbell, confused by the request, flicked the switch.

'Very intimate,' he said, 'will I put some music on?'

West smiled to herself as she directed the FLS over the jacket.

'Why turn the lights off then use a torch?'

'This,' said West, 'is a forensic light source, picks up fingerprints, traces of body fluid...'

'I see. You mean, like blood, or...'

'Anything fluid that comes out of the body.'

'Oh.'

'See, here,' said West, pointing to the collar, 'these spots, that look like they're glowing? My guess is, it's blood; probably spatter from the head wound. Get this off to forensics too, please Iain. Quick as you can.'

'Nae bother. By the way, have you, er, have you noticed a place called The Wherry?' said Campbell, as he bagged and sealed the jacket. 'The Old Wherry Tavern? Just up the street?'

'Fraid not,' said West, 'but then again, I'm not here on a sightseeing trip, am I?'

'No, no, of course not. It's a wee pub, that's all, quiet, no football or music, what you might call cosy, old-fashioned, even.'

'Sounds like my kind of pub,' said West, switching the lights on.

'Really?' said Campbell. 'Well, you know what, I could show you where it is, if you like; it's not far.'

'Oh, yeah, then what?' said West, grinning. 'Ply me with drink when we get there?'

'Och, no, I wasn't... I mean, don't get the wrong idea, I just... well, not unless you wanted to.'

'I'd love to,' said West, 'now get that lot off, we've only got a few days on this and the clock's ticking.'

* * *

Munro breezed in, beaming despite his sodden appearance.

'It's dreich out there,' he said, hanging his coat on the

47

radiator to dry.

'You look pleased with yourself,' said West, 'tea?'

'Aye, thanks Charlie, tea would be most welcome, and yes, I am pleased, we finally have a positive ID.'

'Mrs. Fraser?'

'Aye.'

'How'd she take it?'

'Okay, I think,' said Munro, 'we older folk, we somehow expect it, in a way. Death. So, what's happening here? Have you any news for me?'

'Yup,' said West, 'I'm feeling quite chuffed too. The FLS picked up some staining on the collar of Freida's jacket, could be from the head wound, but then again…'

'Excellent, Charlie.'

'And something else, too. Red hair, caught in the button on the sleeve.'

Munro sat down, sipped his tea and let out a satisfied gasp.

'Red hair, you say?' he said. 'We've not interviewed anyone with red hair.'

'Not yet, so, before you say it, we're looking for a red headed smoker with a penchant for foreign fags.'

'In one, Charlie. In one,' said Munro as he yelled towards the front desk. 'Duncan, a word if I may?'

'Chief.'

'Update, please. Tourists?'

'Nothing, chief,' said Reid, 'no-one from Germany staying anywhere round here. There's a party of six from Jersey staying at The Foresters but I don't suppose that's of any use to us, is it?'

'It is not,' said Munro. 'How about Freida's sister, have you made any progress there?'

'Negative, chief, there's an awful lot of people called Brandt in Schleswig.'

'I imagine there are, Duncan, I imagine there are, but keep on it and let Inspector McGreevy know when you find her, she needs to be told what's happened.'

'Roger, that.'

'Oh, listen, something else,' said Munro, 'sit for a moment, would you. You say Mrs. Fraser's a friend of the family?'

'Aye, that's right,' said Reid.

'Have you known her long?'

'Since a bairn, Da used to work with her, up at the house.'

'Is that so?' said Munro. 'Do you mind me asking, what did he do, exactly?'

'Gardener,' said Reid, 'handyman, you know, fixed things up, here and there.'

'I see. Tell me, would he have known Freida Kappelhoff?'

'You'd have to ask him, chief, but he's not mentioned her. Maybe he left before she arrived.'

'Really?' said Munro. 'So, he left a while back then?'

'Years ago,' said Reid, 'some altercation with the owners, they said they couldnae afford to keep him on, but he reckons there was some kinda conspiracy to kick him out.'

'Sounds rather unfortunate, but he kept in touch with Mrs. Fraser?'

'Oh, aye, he'd still go up to the house to visit, she helped him with his reading and writing, she was good like that.'

'What do you mean, reading?' said Munro.

'He's what they call dyslexic, chief,' said Reid, 'and she was the only one who offered to help when other folk were calling him stupid, but he's not stupid, he just cannae read or write too well. But the practical stuff, like growing plants or building a shed, well, he's your man.'

'Thank you, Duncan, most interesting, really. Listen, do you think your father would mind giving me some advice for the garden back home? It's west facing, very exposed. I'm not having much luck with it.'

'Are you joking me? He'd love it, but I'm warning

you, chief, you'll be there for hours, get him on the subject of plants and he'll not shut up. Drop by, whenever you like.'

'Most kind, Duncan, I will that.'

* * *

Sergeant West drained her cup, coughed politely and, having caught Munro's attention, gestured towards the front desk with a casual flick of the head. Munro was taken aback by the sight of the Fiscal, casually dressed in tight fitting jeans and a leather bomber jacket, sashaying towards him.

'Isobel,' he said, standing to greet her, 'this is a ... surprise.'

'Surprise?' said Crawford.

'Aye, that's the word, surprise.'

'And you don't like surprises?'

'I do not. How can we help?'

Crawford planted herself on the corner of his desk.

'Oh, nothing official, I've the afternoon off and, as I was passing,' she said, with a sly grin, 'I thought I'd drop by. See how the investigation was coming along.'

'It's coming along,' said Munro, 'considering we've only been on it a day or two, we're making progress. Solid progress.'

'Good,' said Crawford, glancing at her watch, 'listen, I was just about to grab a bite to eat, are you...'

'Thanks, Isobel,' said Munro, 'but we're in the middle of something here.'

'Okay, maybe later. If you finish at a reasonable hour, we could always...'

'We could,' said Munro. 'I'll let you know.'

'You do that, James. I look forward to it.'

Munro shook his head and glowered at an amused West as Crawford left the building.

'Think you've got a stalker,' she said, trying her best not to laugh.

'The word that springs to mind is *persistent*.'

'Go on,' said West, 'she's virtually invited you to dinner, you never know, you might enjoy yourself.'

'I don't do enjoyment, Charlie,' said Munro. 'I'm only happy when I'm miserable. Besides, she's a wee bit … urban, for me.'

'What do you mean, urban?'

'Cannae cook and likes shopping.'

'How can you tell?' said West.

'Experience, intuition, a sixth sense.'

'Bit of a chauvinistic statement, you don't even bloody know her!'

'Trust me, Charlie, I'll wager her kitchen is home to 50 different types of pan and not one of them has seen the underside of an egg.'

* * *

Constable Reid, down to his shirt sleeves as the roll call of people named Brandt on the census began to take its toll on his eyesight, shouted from his post on the front desk as the computer pinged an alert.

'Chief! Email, incoming!'

'What is it?' said Munro. 'And does it really warrant such an audible announcement?'

'Possibly, chief. It's the Raiffeisen Bank. We've got that mailing address for Freida's account, you know, statements, cards.'

'Excellent Duncan, excellent. Where is it again?'

'Skelmorlie.'

'Where on earth is Skelmorlie?'

'Not far, 20 minutes, tops. Straight down the coast road, oh, that's odd, it's the caravan park,' said Reid, passing him a print-out of the email.

'Why is that odd, Duncan? Some folk actually enjoy living in a…'

'I'm not disputing that, chief,' said Reid, 'but the park's closed over winter, it's not exactly a permanent place of residence.'

'You're proving yourself to be quite invaluable,

Duncan, you know that? Charlie, we're away lassie, get your coat.'

Chapter 8

The rain, a relentless, fine drizzle, did little to distract from the view as Munro, hands clasped habitually behind his back, gazed contentedly out across the Firth to Arran while West weaved her way betwixt the rows of vacant caravans, looking for any signs of life.

'It's like a ghost town,' she said, her shoulders twitching against the cold. 'Any chance of lunch before I die of boredom?'

Munro smiled.

'Okay,' he said as they turned for the car, 'we'll come back when…'

'Can I help you?'

A lanky figure, dressed head to foot in yellow waterproofs, strode towards them, pulled back his hood and winced as the rain hit his balding head.

'We're not open for a few weeks yet,' he said, 'did you want to book something? I can do that for you, if you like.'

'No, no,' said Munro, 'we were just looking for someone.'

'Like I said, you won't find anyone here for a while yet. Who were you after?'

'Freida,' said West. 'Freida Kappelhoff.'

The man glanced furtively at Munro and covered his head.

'I have to get on,' he said, tersely. 'You know the way out.'

'Just a moment,' said Munro, producing his warrant card, 'D.I. Munro, and this is D.S. West, we need a word.'

'I've nothing to say.'

West, frowning, stared at him inquisitively.

'What are you so scared of?' she said.

'Scared? I'm not scared.'

'Oh, but you should be,' said Munro, fixing him with a steely glare. 'Name?'

'McKenzie,' said the man, unsettled by Munro's demeanour, 'Callum McKenzie.'

'And what is it you do here exactly, Mr. McKenzie?'

'Caretaker. Receptionist. Cleaner. Dogsbody is the phrase most people use.'

'Right. Will we go inside now?' said Munro. 'I tend to get a wee bit unpredictable when I'm wet.'

The caravan, occupying possibly the worst pitch on the site, surrounded by trees with no discernible view, was surprisingly large, with two bedrooms, a kitchen, bathroom and a lounge-cum-dining room cluttered with gardening tools, boots, overalls, piles of paperwork and a chainsaw dangling precariously from a hook in the ceiling. McKenzie made no offer of refreshments but simply removed his jacket, tossed it on the floor by the door and wiped the raindrops from his glasses.

'Nice here,' said West as she pulled on a pair of gloves, and hung his jacket rather than walk over it.

'It'll do,' said McKenzie, 'now, if you don't mind, I have to…'

'Now, what I cannae fathom, Mr. McKenzie,' said Munro, as he surveyed the room, 'is why you're so reluctant to talk to us when we've not even asked you a question yet?'

'No reason, just one of those days. Wrong side of bed,

okay?'

'Okay. So. Freida Kappelhoff. How do you know her?'

'Who says I do?'

'Come, come, Mr. McKenzie,' said Munro, 'let's not waste time here. I want to know why her bank statements are being sent to this address.'

McKenzie scratched his chin and grimaced.

'I'm not sure what you mean,' he said, sheepishly.

Munro sighed and zipped up his jacket.

'You know something, Mr. McKenzie,' he said, 'we all have faults. Personality traits, if you will. Mine is an overwhelming lack of patience, especially when it comes to police work, and having to queue in the supermarket. I get angry. Frustrated. So, Detective Sergeant West is going wait here with you, while I fetch a warrant to search this place, and when I return, I guarantee I will personally turn it upside down.'

McKenzie slumped, defeated, onto the sofa and held his hands aloft.

'No need,' he said, 'okay, no need. You win.'

'Good,' said Munro. 'So, how do you know Freida Kappelhoff?'

McKenzie took a deep breath and sighed.

'We were partners, not married, but we lived together.'

'Here?' said West.

'Eventually, I used to have a place in town.'

'How long were you in a relationship with her?'

'Years,' said McKenzie. 'Ten, twelve. Typical man, I cannae remember exactly.'

'And when did you split?'

'Ages ago. Let's see, Lorna must've been about eleven, so, around eight years ago, I reckon.'

'Lorna?' said Munro.

'Aye, my daughter.'

'She walked out on you and her daughter?' said West.

'Her loss,' said McKenzie. 'Doesnae matter. I've done okay, Lorna's a lovely lassie, doing well for herself.'

'So, Freida worked here too? With you?'

'No, no, Freida hated the cold, she liked her creature comforts too much. She worked up on the estate, in the kitchens. That's where she went when she moved out.'

'Why did she end the relationship?' said Munro.

'Who knows,' said McKenzie, 'probably found some other poor bastard to give the runaround.'

Munro cocked his head.

'Would you care to expand on that, Mr. McKenzie?' he said.

'There was talk, gossip, that she was seeing someone else behind my back. I don't like being made a fool of, Inspector.'

'So the split wasn't amicable?'

'Far from it.'

'See, if I were in her shoes,' said Munro, 'then, in those circumstances, I'd be inclined to telephone my bank right away, inform them of my new address. Why has she never done that? Even after all this time?'

'Ask Lorna, she looks after that stuff. Personally, I think she was waiting till she found somewhere a little more permanent to stay, the lodgings at the house were only meant to be a stop gap.'

'I see,' said Munro, 'and Lorna, where does she stay?'

'Paisley,' said McKenzie, 'she's a good job, works in the Co-Op department store, assistant manager already, would you believe, but she always comes to visit on a Sunday; we have lunch. I like to make sure she gets at least one decent meal a week, not just takeaways and tequila.'

'Very admirable,' said West, 'we need her address please, work too.'

'Aye, okay.'

Munro turned to the window. He smiled as a chink of sunlight broke through the cloud and the rain began to ease.

'Mr. McKenzie,' he said, 'what did you do before you moved here? I mean, why give up a place in town to live on a caravan park. Forgive me for saying so, but you don't strike me as a natural for the outdoor life.'

'I was a teacher. Largs. Secondary school.'

'That's a commendable occupation. What did you teach?'

'English literature.'

'Ah, so you'll be fond of the classics, and a wee bit of poetry, too?'

'Used to be,' said McKenzie, 'let's just say my passion for it has waned over the years.'

'So, why did you leave?'

'Kids. I couldnae take it anymore. See, when I started teaching, there was something called respect, Inspector. Respect for the teachers, they were figures of authority, to be listened to. Then it changed. Society changed. Kids these days get away with murder, and you cannae say anything, you know why? Because it'll infringe their human rights. It's all bollocks. That's why I got out.'

'And you took this job, instead?'

'Only one I could find. Twice the hours and half the pay.'

'Is that why Freida left?'

'Who knows, she didn't exactly leave a detailed explanation.'

'Okay, I think that's it for now,' said West, 'we'll need those bank statements though, if you don't mind.'

'I told you, see Lorna, she has them.'

'Of course she has. Right, we'll be in touch, if we need to.'

'Hold on,' said McKenzie, 'just thinking here, all these questions about Freida, what's going on? Has she done something?'

'No, no, we're looking into what you might call a misappropriation of funds, that's all.'

* * *

Munro lowered the visor against the glare of the sun as the wipers glided lethargically across the windscreen. West buckled up and turned to him.

'Why didn't you tell him?' she said, curiously. 'His daughter's next of kin, if he finds out, you could be in serious shit.'

'If I'd told him, Charlie,' said Munro, staring blankly into space, 'the first thing he'd have done is run to Lorna, then we'd have lost both of them before we even found out what was happening to the money, let alone who killed Freida.'

'Fair enough,' said West, 'still a bit risky though.'

'Not as risky as a bowlful of sushi. Trust me.'

'So, what do you think?' said West. 'Think he's in the frame?'

Munro sighed.

'It's possible, Charlie,' he said, 'it's possible. The motive could be money, I mean, Freida has a pot while he's earning nothing and raising their daughter, but I'm not convinced.'

'He does have red hair.'

'Aye, he does that,' said Munro. 'What there is of it.'

'If we could get a sample of his DNA, we could run a cross-profile with the hairs I found on Freida's jacket, which would prove he'd seen her recently.'

'Aye, but if we ask for a swab, lassie, he'll get suspicious.'

'There is another way,' said West, grinning, as she unfurled her gloved fist.

Munro looked at the short, wispy, red hairs in the palm of hand.

'Where did you...?

'Hood of his jacket,' said West, 'when I picked it up.'

'By jiminy, Charlie, you're a sly fox. Well done lassie. Off to the lab, soon as we're back.'

'Aye, aye, captain. Does that mean we can eat now?'

'Charlie, it will be my pleasure to treat you to the best

haggis toastie in town.'

'I'd rather choke on my own vomit.'

Chapter 9

'Duncan,' said Munro, as they returned to the station, 'wee favour, laddie, go fetch a large bag of chips for Charlie here, she's suffering from malnutrition.'

'Roger that, chief.'

'And when you're back, we've a parcel to go to the lab. Chop, chop.'

Sergeant Campbell, pausing only to shoot a sideways glance at West, leapt from his desk clutching a sheaf of papers.

'Chief, Charlie,' he said, 'I've some news for you on the…'

'Hold on Iain, first things first,' said Munro, 'where's Nick?'

'No idea, chief, I assume he's on a call; he's not checked in yet.'

'Okay, before I forget, fellow by the name of Callum McKenzie, used to be a teacher down in Largs, works at the caravan park in Skelmorlie. I need to know everything about him.'

'Chief.'

'Now, tell me Iain, can you multi-task?'

'Aye, reckon so,' said Campbell, perplexed.

'Good. Tell me your news while you switch the kettle on.'

'Lab report, chief. On the hammer.'

'Go on,' said Munro.

'Get this, it's a shoe hammer. As used by cobblers.'

'Is it, indeed?' said Munro.

'Plus, we've a DNA match off the face – Freida; and, we've some prints,' said Campbell. 'Guess who?'

Munro sat back and stirred the teabag floating in his mug.

'Rudy Kappelhoff,' said Munro, with a sigh.

'Aye,' said Campbell, 'how did you know?'

'It's obvious, Iain. Too obvious,' he said, unimpressed.

'Thought you'd be happy, chief,' said Campbell, perturbed by Munro's less than enthusiastic response, 'I mean, does this not place him at the scene?'

'It does not, Iain. It simply places a hammer belonging to Mr. Kappelhoff at the scene.'

'Right. See what you mean.'

'Nonetheless, we should have a word.'

'Salt and vinegar, miss,' said Constable Reid, half out of breath from his jog to the chippy, 'oh, and I put a sausage in there too, wasn't sure, but, you don't have to eat it.'

'Thanks Duncan,' said West, appreciatively.

'Charlie, let's go,' said Munro, 'you can eat those on the way.'

* * *

Kappelhoff, oblivious to the couple sitting in the car opposite his shop, stood hunched over a jack, wrestling the soles from a pair of riding boots while Munro and West, polishing off the last of the chips, watched in voyeuristic silence.

'It's like being at the cinema,' she said, quietly, 'like watching a silent movie at a drive-in.'

Munro smiled and unclipped his seat belt.

'Shall we?' he said. 'Or are you having dessert?'

Kappelhoff, his bandana drenched with sweat, begrudgingly downed tools and opened the door.

'More questions?' he said, scowling. 'My wife is not yet in the ground but still you come, tormenting innocent peoples.'

'We do our best, Mr. Kappelhoff,' said Munro, holding aloft a plastic bag containing the hammer, 'recognise this?'

Kappelhoff's eyes widened in recognition.

'Mein schlosserhammer!' he said. 'Where did you find this? I have been looking everywhere.'

'You lost it?' said West.

'Yes, a few days ago. I think someone is stealing it.'

'Really?' said Munro, smirking. 'You think someone would come here just to steal an old hammer?'

'People will rob anything, Inspector, even an old man fixing shoes, just to get money for drugs and alcohol.'

'Aye, right enough,' said Munro, 'I'll give you that. You've not had a burglary though, have you?'

'No.'

'And you've not taken your hammer for a walk up Daff Glen?'

'What?'

'Nothing. Tell me, Mr. Kappelhoff, have you had many visitors recently? Just the last few days?'

'Hardly nobody. I have been closed for two days, apart from that, just three peoples are coming.'

'You're sure?' said West.

'I may be old, lady, but there is nothing wrong with my memory.'

'Sorry. Can you remember who they were?'

'Of course,' said Kappelhoff. 'One was a delivery from the supermarket. One was the girl who thinks she is some kind of pop star, but, *Sie leidet unter Größenwahn.*'

'Sorry?'

'A fraud, a fake, she pretends to be wealthy but her

shoes are cheap, imitation leather from China. I tell her I can do nothing with them and she curses me, and then there was the workman.'

'Workman?' said West. 'Is he regular customer?'

'Nein, I have never seen him before.'

'What was he like?' said Munro.

'Quiet. He did not like to have conversations, not even "how are you?" or "nice day today".'

'How did you know he was a workman?' said West.

'He dressed like one, with the yellow coat, and he had tools in his bag, his rucksack.'

'Forgive me, Mr. Kappelhoff,' said Munro, 'but how do you know what he had in his rucksack?'

'I opened it, how else? To put his shoes in. He was taking so long, looking for his wallet.'

'I see, and I don't suppose you have a name for him, or an address, perhaps?'

'Yes, I have everything, always. I write it down, then, if they don't pay me, I go see them with my schlosserhammer. Wait, I have his ticket, here, look: one pair slip-ons, loafers, new heels. Mr. McKenzie from Skelmorlie.'

West resisted the urge to look at Munro and yelp, waiting instead until they'd returned to the privacy of the car.

'Are you thinking what I'm thinking?' she said.

'If it involves Aberdeen Angus and chipped potatoes, then yes,' said Munro as he started the engine, 'otherwise, probably not.'

'It's all too much of a coincidence then, isn't it? I mean, McKenzie turning up, taking the hammer, giving Freida a whack?'

'Aye Charlie, it is,' said Munro. 'See, you have to ask yourself the question why. Why would McKenzie want to kill Freida and then frame Kappelhoff?'

'The money?'

'No, if he wanted to kill Freida for her money, there's

no reason for him to frame Kappelhoff for the murder, is there? I doubt he even knows he was married to her.'

'Okay, but what then?'

'I'm not sure lassie, but McKenzie's covering his arse for some reason, and we need to find out why.'

* * *

'Back so soon?' said McKenzie as he opened the door, 'I'm just having my soup.'

'We'll not keep you long,' said Munro, 'as long as you tell us what we need to know.'

McKenzie returned to the table and dunked a large crust of bread into a bowl of steaming Cullen skink.

'If it's all the same with you,' he said, 'I'd rather eat this before it gets cold.'

'You go ahead,' said West, 'we'd just like to know what you were doing in Inverkip a couple of days ago.'

'Inverkip?' said McKenzie, frowning. 'You mean Greenock. Oh, no, you're right, I stopped by on the way back from McLeans, to pick my shoes up.'

'McLeans?'

'Tool shop in Greenock. Had to get supplies. Screws, trimmer line, that sort of thing, okay?'

West pulled the hammer from her coat pocket.

'Does this look familiar, Mr. McKenzie?' she said.

'Aye! How'd you get that? That belongs to the old fella who fixed my shoes, been meaning to take it back.'

West glanced at Munro, befuddled.

'You admit taking it?' she said.

'I didnae take it,' said McKenzie, wiping his lips with a tea towel, 'I found it, in my bag, when I got back. I reckon he dropped it in by accident when he packed my shoes away. I had it there, on the side, by the window, or at least I thought I did.'

Munro, confounded, scratched the back of his head, and turned to leave.

'One last thing before we go Mr. McKenzie,' he said, 'are you sure you didnae lend the hammer to anyone?

Someone who needed to hang a picture or something, maybe?'

'Aye, positive.'

'And you've not seen anyone who may've just, helped themselves?'

'Don't be daft, the only folk I get to see are the postman and my daughter. It's not a very sociable existence here, Inspector, gets quite lonely in fact.'

* * *

The drive back to Gourock, thought West, with a clear sky above, a rapidly setting sun and an empty carriageway, would have been entirely pleasurable, were it not for the fact that Munro, with his window down, allowed a howling wind to whistle through the car, lowering the temperature to a barely tolerable degree.

'Is that window open for a reason?' she said, sarcastically. 'Or are you deliberately trying to lure me into a state of cryogenic suspension?'

Munro glanced at West, smiled softly and cursed as he simultaneously tried to hit the close button and answer his phone.

'What blethering idiot is trying to call me while I'm driving?' he said, handing it to West. 'See who it is Charlie, and get rid of them.'

'It's the Fiscal,' she said, with a smirk.

'Don't answer it, let it go to…'

'D.I. Munro's phone…'

'Damn it, woman.'

'He's tied up; can I take a message? No, nothing in the diary… yup, I'm sure that'll be fine… okay, no problem, I'll let him know… no, he'll be there, I'll make sure of it. Okay, bye.'

Munro, his lip curled in anticipation of some devastating piece of news, tried desperately to keep one eye on the road whilst glowering at a grinning West.

'What is it lassie?' he said, impatiently. 'What have you done?'

'Nothing. I just… you know.'

'What?'

'Kiplings Bistro, it's near the hotel apparently.'

'What about it?'

'7.30. You've got a dinner date.'

Munro took a deep breath and exhaled slowly.

'Charlie,' he said, 'there is a distinct possibility that you may now be responsible for yet another murder in this town. Excluding your own. Call her back. Cancel it.'

'No, can't make me. Oh, go on James, look, don't think of it as a dinner date, think of it as more of a business meeting, tap her brain, see if knows anything about McKenzie or Freida.'

Munro shook his head in despair.

'Maybe you should come then?'

'Three's a crowd, lover boy. Besides, I'm going to check out the Wherry Tavern.'

* * *

Much to Munro's delight, the bistro, with its spartan furnishings, bright, overhead lights and tightly packed tables, lacked the intimate ambience he'd been dreading, having, as it did, more in common with a café serving up all-day breakfasts than a restaurant with a reputation for first class food. He scoured the throng of excitable diners and blanched at the sight of Crawford, provocatively dressed in a low-cut, black dress more suitable for a night at the opera than a couple of hours in Inverkip, waving from a table towards the back. He forced a polite smile and squeezed his way through the chattering crowd to greet her.

'Isobel,' he said, 'you look…'

'Thank you.'

'I was going to say, *over-dressed*,'

'We can rectify that later.'

'But, I think *delightful* is more appropriate.'

'Shall we order a drink?' said Crawford as the waiter appeared.

'Aye, scotch, large one. Better make it two. Actually, no, on second thought, I'll stick to red. So, tell me Isobel, was there something in particular you wanted to discuss?'

'In a manner of speaking,' said Crawford.

'Is it the investigation?' said Munro, naively intrigued.

'No, not really.'

'Then, I'm afraid I don't understand.'

'You will,' said Crawford, with a sly wink, 'by the time we've finished the second bottle, you will.'

Munro, forfeiting the opportunity of tasting the wine lest it delay the waiter filling his glass, took a large swig and gasped with relief.

'In that case,' he said, 'I'll go first, if you dinnae mind talking shop, that is.'

'Fire away,' said Crawford as she sipped her wine seductively, 'but let's order first, before we lose the waiter.'

Munro tutted and sighed as he hastily perused the menu in search of something that wasn't *foraged*, *harvested*, *deconstructed*, served with a *jus*, *on a bed*, or as part of a *medley*.

'What are you having?' he said, frustrated.

'I'll have the roasted guinea fowl stuffed with porcini mousse, served with a smoked garlic and shallot cream, braised celeriac and Dauphinoise potatoes.'

'Dear God,' sighed Munro. 'See, here,' he said, addressing the waiter, 'this aged sirloin with garlic butter, Parmesan salad and hand-cut, beer-battered chips?'

'Yes, sir.'

'I'll have that.'

'Great.'

'But without the garlic butter.'

'Okay.'

'Or the Parmesan salad.'

'Okay.'

'And can you fill the void on the plate with some extra chips, please. Oh, and make sure it's well-done, I can't abide anything twitching on my plate.'

Crawford smiled as she topped up the glasses.

'I like a man who knows what he wants,' she said, popping a gratuitous olive into her mouth, 'so, go on James, what do you need to know?'

Munro took another large sip of wine.

'The big house, up on the estate,' he said, lowering his voice.

'You mean Dunmore?'

'Aye, that's it. Has anything ever happened there? You know, anything ... untoward?'

'You'd have to ask Nick, he's been here much longer than me, and it's his patch.'

'So, nothing so serious that you would have been involved?'

'Afraid not James,' said Crawford, 'why?'

'Och, no reason,' said Munro, 'I'm fishing really. It's just that Freida worked there, she lived there too, so, maybe she rubbed somebody up the wrong way.'

'Can't help you there, but there is some gossip, Lord knows if it's true; it was a long time ago and you know how Chinese whispers can distort the facts.'

'Okay, go on.'

'All a bit Lady Chatterley really,' said Crawford, mischievously. 'Story goes, the lady of the manor had a fling with one of the staff, the groundskeeper or handyman, something like that.'

'Is that it?' said Munro.

'Not quite. You see, when her husband found out, naturally he was furious and sacked him on the spot, marched him off the estate with a twelve bore to his back but, much to everyone's surprise, there was uproar amongst the staff, the female staff, who demanded he be reinstated immediately.'

'Why was that then? Was he related to them?'

'No,' said Crawford, 'turns out it wasn't just the lady of the house he'd been attending to, he'd been working his way through a few of the other members of staff at the same time. Quite the Lothario, if you ask me.'

'What? And they didn't mind? I mean, that they were … sharing him?'

'Apparently not.'

'Well, well, well. I don't suppose a name comes with all this diluted gossip, does it?'

'I wish it did, someone with that kind of stamina has got to be worth meeting.'

Munro cringed and drained his glass as the meal arrived.

'Let's order another bottle,' said Crawford, 'we've plenty of time to…'

'No, no,' said Munro curtly, as he inspected his steak for signs of blood. 'Sorry Isobel, best not, I've an early start, we've still lots of ground to cover and time's against us. I best take myself off as soon as we've eaten.'

'Okay,' said Crawford, conceding defeat, 'can't say I'm thrilled about it, I was looking forward to a cosy…'

'Maybe once we've closed the case, maybe I could make it up to you then.'

'I'll hold you to that, James.'

'I'm sure you will Isobel. I'm sure you will.'

Chapter 10

The manager, who likened his position to that of the CEO of a multi-national corporation rather than somebody in charge of the day to day running of a local department store, swivelled annoyingly in his leather-backed chair, adjusted the over-sized knot in his tie and smiled cheekily at West.

'Sorry,' he said, 'but like I say, I've only two assistant managers, Keith and Fiona; both hands-on, both with a positive, can-do attitude. There's not a Lorna McKenzie amongst them.'

Munro cringed as the hackneyed phrases grated on his ears.

'What about other members of staff?' he said. 'You know, on the shop floor perhaps? Part-time, temporary even?'

'I know all my staff by name, Inspector. I employ what you might call a personal approach, treat them like we're all one big, happy family. Team players, go-getters, reaching for the moon and pulling down stars…'

'Good grief.'

'I'd know if we had a McKenzie…'

'Hold on,' said West, 'what about Brandt? Have you

anyone on the payroll called Brandt?'

'Brandt?' said the manager, surprised. 'Definitely not, that's not a common name, is it? I'd certainly remember if I had a Brandt on my playlist. Sorry, I cannae be more helpful.'

* * *

'Maybe he got it wrong,' said West as they stood on the street and stared blankly at a three-piece suite in the shop window, 'McKenzie, I mean. Maybe there's another Co-Op round here, somewhere.'

'No, no,' said Munro, 'there's just the one.'

'What about an alias? Think she could be working under an assumed name?'

'No, too complicated Charlie; that would have to involve National Insurance numbers and different bank accounts so her salary could be paid. I cannae see the lassie doing that.'

'Well,' said West, 'looks like someone's leading us a merry dance then.'

'Not just us, Charlie,' said Munro, 'I've a feeling McKenzie has no idea that his daughter's been lying through her front teeth, either.'

'You reckon she's hiding something then?'

'Oh aye, undoubtedly. Peas in a pod, those two. Peas in a pod.'

'Right, shall we try her home address then?'

* * *

The once proud sandstone, tenement building on Broomlands Road, surrounded by betting shops and fast-food outlets, had fallen into a state of mild disrepair. With its dark, anonymous windows and front doors begging for a fresh coat of paint, it was, observed Munro, less than inviting. West buzzed the entry phone.

'Second floor,' she said. 'Walk up.'

'Hello?' came the crackling reply.

'Hello,' said West, 'I'm looking for Lorna, Lorna McKenzie.'

'Who's asking?'

'Police. Nothing serious, we just need a word.'

'What about?'

West hesitated and looked at Munro with a shrug of the shoulders.

'It's about your father, Callum,' he said, 'nothing to worry about, he's not very well, that's all.'

Lorna McKenzie, shrouded in an over-sized dressing gown, stood bare-footed by the open door. With her wayward, flame-red tresses tumbling over shoulders, swollen, puffy eyes, and anaemic complexion, West knew, instinctively, that she'd risen far too early from what must have been a hell of a night.

'What is it?' she said, squinting as though even the pale, yellow light of the single bulb in the hallway was too much to bear. 'Is he okay?'

'Can we come in?' said West, mustering a sympathetic smile.

McKenzie led them to the tiny lounge where she sat at the small dining table, sniffed a tumbler of what looked like water and knocked it back in one.

'So? What's wrong with the numpty?' she said, rubbing her face. 'He's not killed himself has he?'

Munro directed West to the kitchen with a subtle flick of the head and sat opposite McKenzie.

'What makes you say that?' said Munro. 'Does he have suicidal tendencies?'

'I wish.'

'Do you not get on your father?'

'Oh, we get on well enough,' said McKenzie, 'but let's just say he's about as much fun as a fire at a funeral.'

'You don't seem to have much compassion for a fellow who raised you single-handedly, saw to your education, fed and clothed you.'

'Och, I'll give him that, okay, but look at him, up to his knees in mud, cow-towing to a bunch of bampots who lord it up just because they've rented a wee caravan for a week. Treating him like dirt. He should've made something of himself.'

'Like you?' said Munro.

'How'd you mean?'

'Well, assistant manager at the Co-Op, already, and you're not even 20. That's quite an achievement.'

'It is, aye.'

'Only, it's not true is it?' said Munro. 'See, Lorna, we've just come from the Co-Op, and they've never heard of you.'

'Did you go to the right one?' said McKenzie, defensively. 'It's not a wee shop, you know, it's big department store.'

Munro's eyes narrowed as he stared at her unflinchingly.

'Okay,' she said, caving in, 'okay. I said it to keep him happy, get him off my back about getting a job, right?'

West, arms folded, leant casually against the kitchen door and surveyed the debris littering the lounge: the takeaway pizza boxes, the empty juice cartons, the overflowing ashtrays and the discarded clothing with incongruous labels – a dress from Moschino, shoes by L.K. Bennett, a leather shoulder bag embossed with a Ted Baker logo.

'Are you a heavy smoker, Lorna?' she said.

'Me? No, filthy habit, I dinnae smoke myself.'

'The ashtrays are full.'

'Friend of mine, he likes a wee puff now and then.'

'Now and then?' said West, sarcastically. 'Must've been here a while. How'd you get by? Financially, I mean. You're not working, so…'

'I do okay, a bit on the welfare,' said McKenzie, 'and my boyfriend, he helps me out, looks after me.'

'Ah, young love, eh Lorna?' said Munro, forcing a subtle smile. 'What does he do? Take you out clubbing, dancing, that sort of thing?'

'No, he's not into that, he's more refined,

sophisticated, prefers restaurants and wine bars.'

'Quite unusual for a young man these days, I thought he'd be in to…'

'He's not that young, he's … well, he's mature. Divorced.'

'I see.'

'Look,' said McKenzie, 'I don't mean to be rude, but I've a screaming headache and you're here to talk about my Daddy, not me, so what's up? Is he in hospital?'

'No, no,' said Munro, 'he's perfectly healthy, couldn't be better, in fact.'

'Then, what are you…?'

'It's not your father we're here to talk about, Lorna, it's your mother…'

'Oh, aye?'

'Or rather, her finances, her money. In particular, the disappearance of a rather large sum from her bank account.'

What colour there was drained from McKenzie's cheeks as she pulled the dressing gown tight around her body.

'Don't know what you mean,' she said, fumbling with the empty glass.

'Callum told us you take care of your mother's mail, the correspondence from the bank. He told us you pass it on to her.'

'He's lying. Why would I? I'm not a messenger.'

'So, you've nothing here that would be addressed to her?'

'No.'

'Okay,' said Munro, 'we'll double-check with your father, perhaps he got … confused. So, tell me Lorna, when was the last time you saw your mother?'

'I don't recall. It's been a wee while,' said McKenzie hesitantly.

'Roughly speaking,' said Munro, 'a week? A month? Three months, perhaps?'

'Aye, about that. Why?'

'Oh, no reason. Just curious, that's all. One more thing, we need to have a look at your bank statements too, if you don't mind.'

'My bank statements? Why? What for? You're not having those, they're personal. It's none of your business.'

'Oh, but it is, lassie,' said Munro, 'see, you're part of an inquiry now. A fraud inquiry. If you've nothing to hide, then…'

'Can't help. Sorry.'

'Pity, but not to worry, we'll come back with a warrant or simply contact your bank ourselves, get them to send us what we need.'

McKenzie, avoiding eye contact with Munro, laughed nervously.

'Good luck with that, Inspector,' she said, 'but they'll not give them to you, something called the Data Protection Act, I believe.'

'Och, don't you go worrying about wee laws like that. See, I can get whatever I want, lassie. Whatever I want.'

* * *

Munro buckled up and turned to a smug-looking West.

'Come on then,' he said, 'let's have it.'

'Kitchen,' she said, grinning as she held up a small paper bag.

'And that would be?'

'Toothbrush!'

'What?' said Munro. 'Are you some kind of closet kleptomaniac? You cannae go taking…'

'Oh, come on James, we're going to need a profile sooner or later, and we don't have time to fanny around, we've got to do what we can to speed this investigation along.'

Munro shook his head and smiled.

'You've come a long way since we first met, lassie, I'll give you that. Remind me to keep an eye on my wallet next time we're out. What else?'

'Six bottles of Veuve Clicquot in the fridge, an empty in the sink. Watch on the draining board, Tag Heuer. The clothes, all designer. The only thing she's not splashing out on is food.'

'Ah, if there's one thing we Scots know about, Charlie, it's how to maintain a healthy diet.'

'She's lying,' said West, 'how could she afford...'

'Of course she is Charlie, och, she's not fooling anyone, we know that. And the letters from the bank are somewhere in that apartment.'

'So, shouldn't we bring her in? Get a warrant? Search the place?'

'All in good time.'

'But what if we're too late? I mean, what if she destroys them? What if she legs it?'

'Charlie, you worry too much. Trust me, the only place Lorna McKenzie is going, is back to bed.'

'So, what now?' said West.

'Freida's place,' said Munro, 'we need to take a good look around.'

'Bit late for that, isn't it? Besides, I thought Inspector McGreevy was going to take care of that.'

'Oh, I'm sure he will, but you know as well as I do, lassie, the man's a pen-pusher, he wouldn't know trouble if it leapt up and bit him on the face.'

* * *

West contemplated the view across the Clyde as they passed by Langbank, puffed out her cheeks and sighed impatiently at the line of traffic stretching ahead, hindering their progress and delaying, in the absence of breakfast, what she anticipated to be a substantial lunch. The phone call was a welcome distraction.

'It's Sergeant Campbell,' she said, placing the phone on the dashboard, 'I'll put him on speaker, might have some news. Iain, how's it going?'

'Charlie, aye, all good. You okay to talk?'

'Yup, fine, what's up?' said West.

'Oh, I was just wondering what you thought of the Wherry?'

Munro, saying nothing, turned to West and smiled broadly.

'Yeah, it was nice,' she said. 'Quaint.'

'So, you enjoyed yourself then?' said Campbell.

'Had a lovely time.'

'Good, only I was thinking, if you're up for it there's a wee restaurant by the marina, I've not been there myself but I've been meaning to check it out, so, I was wondering...'

'She'd love to, Iain,' said Munro, grinning, 'book a table, I'll make sure she's there.'

'Is that you, chief? Oh, Christ, I thought you were alone, me and my big mouth...'

'Relax,' said Munro.

'My face is burning hot.'

'Sounds great,' said West, giggling, 'so, is that it?'

'No,' said Campbell, wheezing, 'no, it bloody isn't. Christ. Okay, it's Callum McKenzie. Will I go on?'

'Aye,' said Munro, 'if you can stop hyperventilating, that is.'

'Okay. So, Callum McKenzie: age, 48; born, Kilmarnock; educated, University of Strathclyde. Worked as a proof-reader for a while, then on The Herald in Glasgow writing book reviews before moving to Largs where he taught English, language and literature. Seems he was constantly over-looked for promotion to head of department because of his erroneous behaviour.'

'What do you mean?' said West.

'A few complaints along the way, from pupils.'

'Go on.'

'Put it like this, Charlie, he didnae give up his teaching post of his own accord. He left to avoid prosecution.'

'What?'

'Allegations of indecent assault were made against him

by a sixth former.'

'Are you joking me?' said Munro.

'No chief,' said Campbell. 'Naturally, he denied everything, but see, the girl in question wasn't underage, she was 17 at the time, so it was his word against hers, and when push came to shove, she refused to testify; said it was too traumatic.'

'Don't blame her,' said West.

'Aye, so he resigned before it all became public knowledge. Still got his pension though.'

'And now we know why Freida Kappelhoff walked out on him.'

Chapter 11

Apart from a lavish weekend spent languishing in the historical surroundings of Thornbury Castle with a man who was, temporarily, her fiancé, Sergeant West had not the slightest interest in stately homes and readily associated the term "servants' quarters" with cramped accommodation tucked away in the garret at the top of a house, not the sprawling apartment once occupied by Freida Kappelhoff.

'Bloody hell,' she said, gawping at the period fittings, 'if this is how the skivvies live, I can't wait to see the rest of the house.'

Munro, adopting the posture of an avid art connoisseur, studied the gilt-framed paintings adorning the wood-panelled walls and smiled contentedly at a centuries-old rendering of Sweetheart Abbey.

'That's not far from me,' he said. '700 years old and still standing. There's a few builders I know could learn a thing or two from that.'

'I'm sure there are, Inspector,' said Mrs. Fraser, 'now, will I fetch some tea? A sandwich, perhaps?'

'Oh, I wouldn't like to impo…'

'Yes please,' said West, 'if it's not too much trouble.'

Munro, snapping on a pair of gloves, turned on his heels and scanned the room.

'Look around you, Charlie,' he said, arms outstretched, 'what does all this tell you about Freida Kappelhoff?'

'She had class.'

'And? Look around, Charlie. Look and think.'

West smiled knowingly.

'She was neat. Tidy. Organised.'

'Exactly. And organised folk like to file things away. You take the bureau; I'll have a wee nosy through there.'

Munro smiled as he cast an approving eye around the small, yet comfortably furnished bedroom. A rich mahogany tallboy, doubling as a pedestal for a chipped Victorian chamber pot, stood in the corner. A dressing table, bare save for a hand mirror and hairbrush, occupied a space in front of the window. The clothes in the wardrobe were hung, coats to the left, dresses to the right. A collection of woollen sweaters was folded neatly on the top shelf whilst three pairs of shoes, placed regimentally side by side, occupied the lower. He frowned, somewhat disappointedly, at the absence of the mandatory shoebox filled with photographs and mementos of a well-travelled life. West interrupted his search with an enthusiastic cry.

'What is it?' he said, looking over her shoulder.

'It's all here,' said West, engrossed in the contents of a drawer, 'well, almost all. Look, address book, nothing personal in it though, just the dentist, doctor, garage, solicitor and a taxi firm. There's a chequebook and debit card from the RBS; a ScotRail Smartcard; half a dozen ticket stubs, Edinburgh – Frankfurt, Lufthansa; and a camera, but nothing from the Raiffeisen Bank.'

Munro stared blankly at the carpet.

'It's like flat-pack furniture from Sweden,' he said, pensively.

'You what?'

'There's always a missing part Charlie, there's always a

missing part. Let's see that camera, you grab the address book, call the taxi company and see if she's used them recently; then call the solicitor, see if he knows anything that might be relevant.'

'Okay,' said West as Munro switched on the camera and scrolled through the images, 'anything on that?'

'Nothing that'll win the Taylor Wessing prize, just lochs and, oh, there's one here of Nick.'

West stood and glanced over Munro's shoulder.

'That looks quite recent,' she said, 'go on, any more?'

Munro flicked through the next four frames, stopping at a picture of Freida sitting on a dry stone wall, holding hands with a shy-looking man dressed in a tweed jacket.

'I wonder who...' said West, cut short as Fraser entered the room.

'Now then,' said Mrs. Fraser as she set a large, silver tray atop the dining table, 'come sit, there's roast beef, or gammon if you prefer, plenty of mustard and some apple sauce.'

West, needing no second invitation, bounded to the table and eagerly tucked in.

'You're a lifesaver, Mrs. Fraser,' she said, 'thank you so much. I was expecting cucumber sandwiches with the crusts cut off.'

'This is Dunmore House, dear, not Buckingham Palace. Now, who's for tea?'

'Thank you,' said Munro. 'Mrs. Fraser, I notice Freida has a telephone number for a garage in her address book? Do you know where she keeps her car?'

'Oh, she doesn't have a car, Inspector, I let her borrow mine from time to time. If she wanted to go shopping, that sort of thing. I have her on my insurance.'

'I see. She's not much in the way of possessions, has she?' said Munro. 'Things of a personal nature, I mean.'

'No,' said Mrs. Fraser. 'If there were two things Freida detested with a passion, Inspector, it was clutter and dust.'

'Even so, the apartment is awfully well-kept. Are you

sure the cleaner's not been in since … since Freida passed on?'

'We are the cleaners,' said Mrs. Fraser.

'Anyone else?'

'No, well, the police of course, they were here, not long after you'd dropped me back from the mortuary.'

'They've been already? And you were here at the time?' said Munro.

'I was. It was Mr. McGreevy and a young officer.'

'McGreevy? You know Inspector McGreevy?'

'Oh yes, we go back a long way.'

'See here, Mrs. Fraser,' said Munro, producing the camera, 'that explains this picture of Nick here, but would you happen to know who this is, next to her on the wall?'

Mrs. Fraser took the camera, held it at arm's length and squinted.

'Och, that's Donald,' she said, pushing the camera away with an air of disgust, 'young Duncan's father.'

'I see,' said Munro, intrigued by her reaction, 'and did he and Freida see a lot of each other?'

'More than was healthy, if you ask me, but I'll say no more on the subject.'

'Okay, fair enough.'

'About the police,' said West, sipping her tea, 'were they here long?'

'I'd say it was hardly worth them coming, dear.'

'And why's that?' said Munro.

'Well, it wasn't like you see on the television, they didn't spend hours turning the place upside down. No, they opened a few drawers, looked under the bed, checked the waste paper baskets, that sort of thing, and that was it.'

'And there's been no-one else?' said West.

'No, not since, but … but there was the night Freida went to meet her gentleman friend in Inverkip, the night she never came back.'

'Someone came to see Freida?'

'Not exactly, I'm not sure what…'

'Did you meet them?'

'In a manner of speaking.'

'Go on,' said Munro, quietly, 'and think carefully, Mrs. Fraser, try and remember everything.'

'Well, like I said, it was the night Freida went to Inverkip. It was late.'

'How late?'

'Past midnight. Closer to 1am, I think. I was about to turn in when I heard a noise next door. Well, I assumed it was Freida, back from her night out, so I went to see. I thought perhaps I'd make us some cocoa, it was dreich out, I thought she'd appreciate that.'

'And?'

'It wasn't Freida, of course. Gave me quite a scare though; I mean, I thought it was a burglar.'

'You thought?' said Munro. 'So, it wasn't? It was someone you knew?'

'No,' said Mrs. Fraser, 'I'd never seen her before.'

'Her?' said West.

'That's right, young lass, student type; you know, anorak, jeans and a rucksack – said she was her daughter.'

'Daughter?' said Munro. 'And was she?'

'Of course not,' said Mrs. Fraser, shaking her head. 'Not once, in all the time I've known her, did Freida ever mention a daughter. A sister, yes, back home. But not a daughter.'

'What happened next?'

'I told her to leave; leave and be thankful I wasn't calling the police. And she did, in a hurry.'

'Could you describe her, Mrs. Fraser?' said West.

'I doubt it, dear. It was dark, she was wearing a hood.'

Munro stood abruptly.

'Mrs. Fraser,' he said, smiling warmly, 'your hospitality has been generous to a fault, but we have to go now. Before we do, I must ask you lock this door and not open it for anyone, is that clear?'

'Aye, okay, Inspector. Will you be coming back then?'

'Not us, Mrs. Fraser, some colleagues from forensics, we'll have to give this place a good going over.'

'Like they do on the television?'

'Aye, like that.'

* * *

West struggled to keep up as Munro, uncharacteristically flustered, marched determinedly back to the car.

'Okay, Charlie,' he said, not pausing for breath, 'why weren't we told McGreevy was here?'

'Dunno, maybe he's not got round to telling you yet?'

'No, no, listen, you need to call forensics now; get them up here as soon as possible. In the meantime, I want the room sealed off, got that?'

'Got it.'

'Then organise a warrant for McKenzie's flat.'

'You think it was her? In the flat?' said West.

'I'm not a betting man, Charlie, but I'd wager a fiver she owns an anorak and a rucksack.'

'Shall we bring her in too?'

'Not till we've searched the place,' said Munro as he revved the engine and sped down the drive, 'I need to have a wee chat with Constable Reid's father first; he used to work here, he might be able to…'

West lurched forward, saved by the seatbelt, as Munro slammed on the brakes and stared, momentarily, through the windscreen, before throwing the car into reverse and haring back towards the house.

'What's up?' said West. 'What have you…?

'Come Charlie, quick,' said Munro, leaping from the car.

* * *

'Back so soon, Inspector?' said Mrs. Fraser. 'Did you forget…'

'No, no. We need to see Freida's apartment again, won't take long.'

'Of course. Is there anything I can do to help?'

'Oh, you've done enough Mrs. Fraser. If I'm right, then you are heaven sent.'

'Whatever do you…?'

Munro went straight to the bedroom and pointed to the mattress.

'Charlie,' he said, 'take that end. Now lift, high as you can.'

West, speechless, stared at the large, manila envelope lying on the box-spring.

'Don't just stand there, lassie,' said Munro, impatiently, 'pick it up.'

West snatched the envelope and tipped the contents onto the bed. A wad of papers, all bearing the Raiffeisen logo, and two bank cards.

'You're a bloody genius,' she said, exasperated, 'how did you know?'

Munro walked to window and took up his customary stance, hands clasped behind his back, as he pondered the implications.

'I suppose this means Lorna McKenzie was telling the truth after all,' said West ruefully, 'that's a bit embarrassing, isn't it? Still, I suppose…'

Munro turned and looked at West, stony faced.

'It's not embarrassing at all, Charlie,' he said, his voice menacingly low, 'see, the lassie Mrs. Fraser disturbed, the intruder …'

'Lorna McKenzie.'

'… possibly, probably, Lorna McKenzie, she wasnae here to rob the place.'

'What do you mean?' said West. 'Why else…'

Munro pointed to the envelope in her hand.

'She was here to put something back.'

Chapter 12

'On your own, miss?' said Constable Reid as West approached the desk. 'Where's the chief?'

'On his way to see your Dad, Duncan, something about gardening tips. Now, I need this sent to the lab for a profile,' she said, handing him the toothbrush, 'and tell them it's urgent, like yesterday urgent.'

'Roger that.'

'Oh, and forensics are on their way to Freida's place, Dunmore House, chase them too please. Iain, how's it going?'

Sergeant Campbell, mortified, glanced up at West and smiled nervously as he self-consciously toyed with a desk stapler.

'You could have told me he was with you,' he said in a loud whisper, 'I thought you were on your own.'

'Don't worry, bashful!' said West.

'But I do, Charlie. He's going to be watching me like a hawk now, in case I upset his D.S.'

'And will you?'

'What? No, no, of course not,' said Campbell, 'all I'm saying is, Christ, it's like having a father-in-law when you're not even married.'

'I know! Great, isn't it? So, have you booked this highfalutin, fancy restaurant yet?'

'No, not yet. I'll do it later.'

'Probably quite pricey isn't it?' said West.

'Aye, but it's quality food, Charlie, I mean, you don't get pearls for the price of paste. It'll be nice, you know…'

'Romantic?'

'No, not … well, Christ you're as bad him.'

'Tell you what, save your money, I've a better idea.'

'What's that then?'

'Pub,' said West, smiling, 'few pints and a fish supper, we can eat at yours.'

'Really?' said Campbell, pleasantly surprised. 'You're up for that?'

'Well, we could get a kebab instead, if you want.'

'No, no, that's great Charlie. Perfect.'

* * *

Having never housed a car, the garage – a cold, brick-built affair with wooden, double doors – served as both a potting shed and a workshop, was packed to overflowing with sacks of compost, plant pots, an assortment of tools and gardening equipment, and enough timber to build a ranch. Donald Reid, dressed in a pair of filthy, oil-stained jeans and a thick, roll-neck jumper, was perched on an upturned fruit crate, cleaning the carburettor he'd removed from a lawnmower. Munro tapped the open door.

'Mr. Reid?' he said. 'Duncan said I'd find you here.'

Reid looked up and removed the cigarette dangling from his lips.

'Duncan?'

'Aye. James Munro. I'm working with your son, temporarily.'

'Is that so?' said Reid, suspiciously. 'And what is it you do, exactly, Mr. Munro?'

'James, please. I'm a detective. Detective Inspector actually.'

Reid stubbed out the cigarette and turned his

attention to the carburettor.

'Is there trouble afoot, Inspector?' he said. 'Have you come to interrogate me?'

'No, no,' said Munro, laughing politely, 'I'm not here on official business, it's just that Duncan tells me you're somewhat gifted when it comes to things of a horticultural nature.'

Reid perked up, smiled broadly and held out his hand.

'You'll be wanting some advice then?' he said.

'Only if you have the time, if I'm not disturbing you.'

'Pull up a… something. Make yourself comfortable, if you can.'

'Much obliged,' said Munro, opting to lean, instead, against the workbench.

'So, how can I help?'

'It's my garden, down in Carsethorn. I've tried my best, but I cannae get anything to grow, nothing that lives for more than a few months, that is.'

'Is it west facing?' said Reid, frowning as he pictured the location in his mind's eye.

'Aye, it is.'

'Exposed, no doubt.'

'Very.'

'So, plenty of sun.'

Munro laughed.

'Aye. On a good day.'

'What are you after?' said Reid. 'Trees? That'll give you shade and act as a windbreak, take a wee while to establish though.'

'No, no,' said Munro, 'I was thinking, low maintenance, shrubbery mainly, and some colour. Jean always did like colour.'

'Jean?'

'My wife. Late wife.'

Reid sighed and nodded understandingly.

'Okay,' he said, 'if Jean liked colour, Inspector, then that's what she'll get. Problem with your garden, see, is the soil; gley and peaty. Your options are limited but it's not impossible. I'd plant Rhododendrons and Camellia, that'll take care of the shrubs, then, for a blaze of colour, California Poppies, Geraniums, Cornflower, and some Stocks and Red Hot Pokers for a bit of height. It wouldnae do any harm to add some herbs too, get a nice wee scent in the garden, you know, easy stuff: Lavender, Thyme, Rosemary. Oh, and don't forget the Heather, it's hardy, and the bees'll thank you for it.'

'All that,' said Munro, impressed, 'just off the top of your head? You've a talent there, Mr. Reid, aye, a talent alright. I'll have to write that down. They must miss you up at Dunmore. Sorry, Duncan told me you used to work there, that's how I...'

'Aye, I did. It was great too, Inspector; best job I ever had. Not only did I get to tend the gardens but I built stuff too. The treehouse, for example, that's still there.'

'So, forgive me for asking, but if the job was that great, what on earth possessed you to leave?'

Reid glanced at Munro and hesitated before answering.

'The laird, he didn't... he didn't like the way I ... fraternised with other members of staff.'

'Och, that is a shame,' said Munro, 'it being such a short drive away too.'

'Drive? I dinnae drive, Inspector, on account of my dyslexia, cannae read the signs.'

'I see. Tell me, do you stay in touch with anyone there? You must have forged a good friendship or two over the years.'

'Oh aye, Mrs. Fraser, naturally, and Freida, of course. Cigarette?' said Reid, offering the pack.

'I don't, thanks. Unusual, that's not a brand I've seen before.'

'German,' said Reid. 'Freida brings them for me, when she visits her sister.'

'That's very generous of her.'

'She's a generous lady. Heart of gold.'

'Look, I know it sounds like I'm going off on a tangent here,' said Munro, 'but you may able to help me with something else. Are you familiar with Daff Glen, Mr. Reid?'

'Daff Glen? What dog walker isn't?'

'You've a doggie?'

'Molly. Fox Terrier. But we don't go this time of year, it's too wet, too boggy, she gets herself in a right... hold on, that's where they found a body, right? In the burn?'

'Aye,' said Munro, plainly surprised, 'that's right, but how did... did Duncan...?'

'No, he never tells me anything,' said Reid, 'says it's something to do with the Official Secrets Act. No, it was the fella down the way there. He's a Lab called Buster. Said there was a lassie floating in the water not long ago.'

Munro rubbed his chin and sighed.

'There was indeed, Mr. Reid. Look, there's no easy way of saying this, so you'll excuse me, I'm sure, if I sound blunt, but the body we pulled from the burn, it was... it was Freida Kappelhoff.'

Reid froze and regarded Munro with a look of consternation.

'What?' he said quietly, visibly distressed.

'I'm afraid, it appears she may have...'

'No. Not Freida, surely not... Freida? What, what happened?'

'We're looking into it,' said Munro, 'it's too early to...'

'What would she be doing in the glen? She'd never...'

'You're saying it's out of character?' said Munro.

'Aye, too right it is,' said Reid. 'Freida panicked if she got so much as a speck of dirt on her shoes, she'd never go walking a place like that.'

'Not even as a short-cut perhaps? If she was going...'

'Absolutely not. Hold on,' said Reid, drawing heavily on his cigarette, 'this was no accident, was it? I mean, you're a detective. Why else would a detective be...?'

'No,' said Munro, sighing, 'we don't think it was an accident, Mr. Reid.'

'You're saying she was… now, who would want to do that to Freida? That would be like trying to kill Mother Teresa. The woman's not a bad bone in her body. Christ. Do you know who…?'

'No. Not yet, but we're working on it, trust me, we're doing everything we can. I'll make sure Duncan keeps you informed. Are you okay?'

'No. No, I'm not Inspector. I'm devastated.'

'Understandably,' said Munro. 'Mrs. Fraser was inconsolable herself. Do you think you might see her? As you know each other, like?'

Reid wiped his hands vigorously on a rag and turned to go.

'No,' he said, 'No. I don't think so.'

'Is something the matter, Mr. Reid?'

'Och no, she's alright, it's just … she's a wee bit *clingy*, that's all.'

'Clingy?'

'Aye. Needy. Look, we had a thing, a while back, she and me, before I was married, and she's never got over it.'

'I see. A case of unrequited love.'

'Unrequited love? Pest more like.'

* * *

Munro pulled up outside the station, lowered the window and watched as McGreevy, wearing a pained expression, dawdled up the street, a brown, takeaway cup in each hand.

'Duncan's coffee not to your liking anymore, Nick?' he said, smirking.

McGreevy winced.

'I'm afraid, talented as he is, James, Constable Reid's skills do not extend to double espressos, and neither do our facilities.'

'Must've been a heavy night. I hope she was worth it.'

'I should be so lucky,' said McGreevy, diffidently, 'I

foolishly agreed to a wee bevvy with MacDougal at the marina – details about the regatta.'

'And one pint led to another.'

'No James, one pint led to seven, and I cannae remember the last time I did that. Anyway, how's progress? I've had the Fiscal on the phone asking for you.'

'That's very ... sociable ... of her. We're getting there.'

'Okay, just keep an eye on the clock, we've not much time left.'

'Don't you worry now, I've set the alarm. Do me a wee a favour when you step inside, tell Charlie to get her arse in gear, we've someone to see.'

* * *

'Have you seen the state of him?' said West as she jumped in the car. 'Looks like he's been on a right bender.'

'That's one way of putting it,' said Munro, 'apparently he had a few drinks with the chap who runs the yacht club last night. Mr. MacDougal.'

'Apparently?'

Munro glanced knowingly at West.

'Mr. MacDougal,' he said, 'is a member of the Temperance Society.'

'Ah, someone's been a naughty boy then. I wonder who she is?'

'Charlie, I'm disappointed, that's awfully cynical of you.'

'Only saying what you're thinking.'

'You and I have too much in common.'

'I'll take that as a compliment. So, how was Duncan's dad?'

Munro, saying nothing, stared pensively through the windscreen.

'What's up?' she said. 'What's rankling you?'

'Something Isobel mentioned over dinner,' said Munro, perturbed.

'Go on.'

'There was a chap who used to work at Dunmore, years ago. He was fired for having an affair with the lady of the house.'

'So?'

'And at least one other member of staff.'

'Sly old fox,' said West, grinning.

'It was the gardener. Duncan's father, to be precise.'

'What? You are kidding?' said West, exasperated. 'Does Duncan…?'

'I've no idea, and I'm not about to tell him either.'

'Duncan's dad putting it about, who'd have… hold on, do you think Freida may have been the other…?'

'It's possible, lassie,' said Munro, 'it's certainly possible. There's something else, too. Mr. Reid is a smoker. Same brand as those we found in the glen.'

'Holy crap, then we have to bring him in, surely? I mean…'

'There's just one thing stopping me.'

'Well, come on,' said West, 'out with it.'

'He doesnae drive.'

'What's that got to do with the price of eggs?'

'What need would he have for anti-freeze?' said Munro.

West slumped in her seat, flummoxed.

'Well, I suppose he could, I mean, if he really wanted to, he could easily…'

'No, it doesnae add up Charlie,' said Munro, starting the car, 'see, if you buy anti-freeze when you have no need for it, especially in a place like this, all you'll do is draw attention to yourself. No, whoever poisoned Freida had it to hand. No offence to Mr. Reid, but this is out of his league. It's too clever by half.'

'Callum McKenzie would need it though,' said West, 'and he's clever, and he has red hair.'

'Aye lassie, I know, but he doesnae have the piece of the jigsaw with cigarette stamped on it. But his daughter might. Have you got the warrant?'

'Yup.'

'Okay. And listen, not a word to young Duncan, understand?'

* * *

A bedraggled McKenzie, still swathed in her gown and wearing a face like thunder, opened the door and glowered at Munro.

'I am sorry,' he said, glibly, 'I thought you'd be up by now. How's the head?'

McKenzie sneered.

'Nobody likes a smartarse, Inspector,' she said.

'No, they do not, lassie. Least of all, me.'

'So, come on, what is it now?'

West, holding up the search warrant, brushed her aside and entered the flat.

'Let's take a seat while Detective Sergeant West here, has a wee look around.'

'What? Oh no you don't,' said McKenzie, chasing her to the lounge, 'you touch anything and I'll…'

'You'll do nothing,' said West, sternly, 'but I'll do you for obstruction. Now, sit.'

Munro, smiling like a proud father, opened the curtains and sat opposite McKenzie at the table.

'I'd stay on the right side of her, if I were you,' he said, 'I can guarantee her bite is much worse than her bark. Now then, where shall we start? Oh yes, bank statements.'

McKenzie sat back and folded her arms.

'You've got the warrant, Inspector,' she said, defiantly, 'you find them.'

Munro, unsettling McKenzie with his penetrating gaze, spoke without averting his eyes.

'Charlie,' he called, 'Miss McKenzie here says she not bothered if you make a mess, she'll tidy up afterwards.'

'Nice try Inspector, but you don't frighten me, I'm still not…'

'In that case,' said Munro, 'Lorna McKenzie, I'm arresting you on suspicion of…'

'What? Are you joking me?'

'Theft and obtaining goods by deception, you…'

'Alright! Okay. Hold on, hold on. I'll fetch them.'

McKenzie went to the sideboard, produced a pile of unopened letters, and reluctantly slapped them on the table.

'You must be terribly well off,' said Munro as he opened one, 'not checking the state of your finances. I have to check mine every month.'

McKenzie nibbled nervously at her nails as he silently scanned the first, then opened a second, then a third, and then a fourth.

'Well,' he said, replacing them neatly atop the pile, 'there's nothing untoward there, Miss McKenzie, so I fail to see what you were so worried about. Unless, of course, it's something to do with your welfare payments. A false claim, perhaps?'

McKenzie's face flushed.

'No matter,' said Munro, 'I'm not here for that. Now, next thing, would you happen to own a burgundy-coloured coat, by any chance? Like an anorak?'

'Aye. What of it?'

'Does it have a hood?'

'Of course, it has a hood,' said McKenzie, raising her eyes to the ceiling and cursing under her breath, 'it's an anorak, for Christ's sake.'

'And a rucksack?'

'What?'

'It's like a wee bag,' said Munro, sardonically, 'but with straps, so you can…'

'I know what a bloody rucksack is.'

'Well, do you have one?'

'Yes. You're welcome to it; if you can find it.'

'Could you describe it?'

'It's black!' said McKenzie. 'It's a bloody black rucksack. Okay?'

West returned to the room, shook her head, cleared a

space on the sofa and sat down.

'Where were you last Friday, Lorna?' she said. 'Between the hours of 10pm and 3am?'

'Can't remember,' said McKenzie.

'So, you weren't here?'

'Can't remember.'

'With your boyfriend, maybe?'

'Can't remember.'

'Have you had an accident recently?' said Munro. 'A wee fall perhaps?'

'No,' said McKenzie, her bravado waning, 'why?'

'Amnesia. It's often associated with a bump to the head.'

'A comedian too. Very funny.'

'So is the cure, lassie. So is the cure. Now, where was I? Oh yes, Lorna McKenzie, I'm arresting you on suspicion of theft, fraud and obtaining goods by deception. I may add to the list a little later, we'll see how we go. You do not have to… och, I'm sure you're familiar with the rest. Now, get dressed. Chop, chop.'

Chapter 13

McGreevy, having imbibed enough coffee to induce a mild heart attack, sported an enthusiastic grin and watched, wide-eyed, as West and Munro hauled their suspect to the front desk for Constable Reid to book in.

'Duncan,' said Munro, 'would you take care of our guest please, and make sure she's comfortable.'

'Roger that, chief,' said Reid. 'Can you confirm your full name please, Miss?'

'McKenzie. Lorna McKenzie.'

'And how long will you be staying?'

'What?'

'Is it hand luggage only, or do you have any bags to check?'

'Are you for real?'

* * *

'So,' said McGreevy as he clapped his hands, and shuffled back and forth like an amateur tap-dancer, 'is that her? Is that your suspect? Has she confessed? Will I telephone Isobel and give her the good news?'

'Do you need the bathroom, Nick?' said Munro. 'You appear to be awfully agitated.'

'No, I've been. Several times. So, how about it, James?

Will I call her or… no, actually, you should be the one to make the call, I wouldn't want to steal your…'

Munro waved his hand and sat, exhausted, at his desk.

'Nick, we've still not interviewed her,' he said, 'we've a way to go, just yet.'

'Okay. Well, listen, Iain's been climbing the wall…'

'Him as well? Are you two on something?'

'He's tried calling you,' said McGreevy, 'results came in from the lab.'

West checked her phone. Four missed calls.

'Oh, yeah,' she said, 'aw, sweet.'

'Sweet?' said Munro.

'He sent a text as well, put a little smiley face at the end of the message.'

'Good grief.'

Sergeant Campbell, clutching an envelope in one hand and a pint of milk in the other, bounded round the desk.

'Chief! Charlie!' he said. 'I've been trying to reach you; I've got the…'

'Results from the lab?' said West.

'Aye, that's right. How did you… no matter, listen, you won't believe…'

'By Jiminy, Iain!' said Munro, as he thumped the desk, 'will you calm yourself! You're like a love-struck puppy with ADHD.'

'Sorry chief,' said Campbell, 'I just cannae contain myself, see…'

'Haud yer wheesht! Now, first things first. Kettle. Two brews, strong. Quick as you like, or Charlie here will be grounded tonight.'

West smiled as Munro shot her a wink.

'So, Nick,' he said as McGreevy joined them at the table, 'I take it you know forensics were over at Freida's place this morning? Have they any news for us yet?'

'Nothing yet James, what exactly is it you're searching for?'

'If I knew that, do you not think I'd look myself?

Favour please, Nick, ask Duncan to give them a wee nudge before he clocks off. We have to move on this.'

'Here you go,' said Campbell as he eagerly slammed two mugs of murky, milky water on the table, 'needs to steep for a minute or two…'

Munro regarded the tea with a look of revulsion and pushed it to one side.

'Right, Iain,' he said, 'go.'

'Okay. Let's get the bad news out of the way first,' said Campbell, 'Callum McKenzie, he's off the radar. The hair you pulled from his hood, Charlie, it matches nothing.'

'You're kidding?' said West. 'Bummer. I could've sworn he'd be in with a shout, I mean…'

'Hold on,' said Campbell, 'no need to be disappointed just yet. We have two matches for the hair you found snagged on Freida's coat.'

'Two?' said Munro. 'How can that be?'

'You won't believe it, chief. Get this, the first is Lorna McKenzie. The hair matches the DNA sample they got from her toothbrush. So…'

'So, what?' said West. 'Come on, Iain, we don't have time…'

'So, that places her at the scene of the crime, right? In the glen?'

Munro wiped his brow and gritted his teeth in frustration.

'Have you heard of deja-vu, Iain?' he said, agitated. 'It places the hair at the scene. Hair that could have become entangled round that button anywhere, at Freida's apartment, for example.'

'At least we know Lorna was with Freida at some point recently,' said West, 'that's something.'

'Aye,' said Munro, losing the will to live. 'Now, Iain, before you try my patience any further, get on with it.'

'Chief. This one'll get you, the second match…'

'For God's sake, Iain! I'll crucify you in a moment!'

'Kappelhoff,' said Campbell, recoiling. 'The second match. It's Rudy Kappelhoff.'

The room fell silent. West stared at Munro in disbelief.

'And they're absolutely certain about this?' she said, quietly. 'There's no room for error, there's no way they could have…'

'If this was a paternity suit,' said Campbell, solemnly, 'it would be *case closed*. There's no doubt about it Charlie, Rudy Kappelhoff is Lorna's father.'

Munro heaved a sigh, hauled himself to his feet and, hands behind his back, circled the desk at a slow, measured pace. West recognised the sombre expression on his face and allowed him to complete a full circuit before speaking.

'So,' she said, thinking aloud, 'if Freida knew she was pregnant, why walk out on Rudy? I mean, why leave your husband just when you're going to need him most?'

Munro stopped and addressed the ceiling.

'I'll tell you why,' he said, 'because she didn't know it was his. She thought she'd fallen pregnant by Callum McKenzie and had no choice but to leave.'

'I don't get it,' said West, 'surely she could've talked it through, I mean, by all accounts she was clever, intelligent, level-headed…'

'And old-fashioned. She had dignity.'

'Okay, but what about the hair? The red hair? Neither Rudy nor Freida have red hair.'

'No,' said Munro, 'but I can guarantee one of their grandparents did. It's a generational thing. Genetic characteristics have a habit of repeating themselves every three generations.'

McGreevy, looking like he'd won the lottery, headed for his office.

'I have to make a call,' he said, smiling smugly, 'shan't be long.'

Munro watched as he slipped gingerly from the room and closed the door.

'Iain,' he said, 'make sure you've some kitchen towel to hand.'

'Kitchen towel, chief?' said Campbell. 'Why?'

'Because before too long, your boss is going to have egg on his face. Now, as a reward for your rather enthusiastic contribution to this inquiry thus far, I shall allow you to treat D.S. West here, to a libation or two after work. Have her home by 9pm.'

'9pm? Aye, okay chief,' said Campbell with a laugh, 'very funny.'

'Oh, I'm not joking, Iain. I'm certainly not joking. Charlie, let's pop downstairs. It's high time we had a proper chat with Lorna.'

Chapter 14

McKenzie shifted uncomfortably in her seat, unnerved by her surroundings. The interview room, with its high ceiling, large windows and whitewashed walls was not what she'd expected. It was bare, save for the table and chairs they occupied. She cowered as Munro gave her a withering look from across the desk.

'It's late,' she said, meekly, 'are you charging me with anything?'

'Not yet,' said West.

'Then I want to go home.'

'All in good time.'

'You cannae keep me here, you know.'

Munro took the voice recorder from his pocket and placed it carefully on the desk.

'Oh, but we can, lassie,' he said without looking up, 'we can keep you here for twelve hours, and, if you're very lucky, and behave yourself, we can extend that to 24.'

'Then I want a lawyer,' said McKenzie, 'so's I don't incriminate myself.'

'Okay,' said Munro, 'but, see here Lorna, you requesting a lawyer suggests to me that you've something to hide but, it's up to you. You are entitled to one. Now, shall we appoint one for you, or can you afford your own? Och, how silly of me, of course you can. You're loaded.'

McKenzie glanced nervously around the room.

'Forget it,' she said, 'I can take care of myself.'

Munro pressed a button on the voice recorder.

'For the benefit of the tape, present at the interview are Miss Lorna McKenzie, D.S. West and Detective Inspector James Munro. So, Lorna, do you understand why you're here?'

'Aye,' said McKenzie, 'you're falsely accusing me of being a thief. Of robbing my own mother. Of taking money I never knew she had from a bank in Germany I've never heard of.'

Munro paused and smiled gently.

'Lorna,' he said softly, 'we never said it was a German bank. Now, last Friday, were you, or were you not, in Daff Glen?'

'No.'

'You're sure now? Positive?'

'Yes.'

'Because your mother was.'

'Good for her,' said McKenzie.

'Actually, no, it wasn't,' said Munro, 'it wasn't good at all. But see, we found your hair, snagged around a button on her jacket…'

'So?'

'The jacket she was wearing…'

'Means nothing.'

'The night she died.'

'Ouch,' said West, flinching.

McKenzie swallowed hard.

'Sorry,' said Munro, 'I didn't mean to be so blunt, but I'm afraid your mother's passed on.'

'Oh, well,' said McKenzie with a spurious smile, 'we've all got to go, sooner or later.'

'Thing is, Lorna. She didn't die of natural causes.'

'Like I said.'

West leaned forward and frowned curiously.

'You don't seem that concerned,' she said, 'or even shocked.'

'What do you expect?' said McKenzie. 'We weren't close. She walked out on us, remember? Left us to rot in a stinking caravan park while she was in clover.'

Munro leaned back, folded his arms and stared at her, his eyes narrowing like a hawk sharpening its focus before diving for a kill.

'What were you doing at Dunmore House last Friday?' he said.

McKenzie turned her attention to what was left of her fingernails.

'Don't know what you're talking about,' she mumbled.

'You were seen. Wearing your anorak, with your rucksack on your back.'

'I don't believe this; how many times do I have to tell you? I wasn't…'

'Do you have a set of keys?' said West.

'What?' said McKenzie.

'The keys. To your mother's apartment. Where are they?'

'I…'

'Because there's no other way you could have got in without disturbing someone in the house. And your mother didnae have her keys with her when she was found.'

'Maybe she forgot them. Amnesia,' said McKenzie facetiously, 'probably runs in the family.'

'Do you know what I think?' said West. 'I think you were in the glen last Friday. I think you met your mother. I think you argued and had a bit of a tussle and that's how come your hair was caught on her jacket. And I think you killed her…'

'No!'

'I think you killed her and took her keys…'

'No! I didn't do it, I'd never…'

'… and went to Dunmore House to…'

'I'm telling you!' said McKenzie, 'she was still my Mammy, I'd never do that! I could never … look, okay. I saw her, right. We used to meet, now and then, but I was never comfortable with it. We were strangers and she wanted to be close, be a loving, caring parent. It made me sick, playing happy families after what she'd done.'

'Would you like a drink of water?' said West.

'No,' said McKenzie, 'I'd like a large, bloody vodka.'

Munro allowed a brief pause to hang in the air.

'So,' he said, 'the money?'

McKenzie glanced at West and smiled nervously.

'Couple of years back,' she said, 'it was just after my birthday, my eighteenth. The crappiest birthday ever, I couldnae afford to go out, sat indoors all night watching the telly with my Daddy. Do you know what he got me for my birthday? For my eighteenth bloody birthday? A card. That was it. A bloody card. Anyway, there was all this post piling up addressed to Mammy, most of it from the bank, so I opened one. I opened one and nearly bloody cried, I mean, my Daddy had always said she was minted, but this was unbelievable. I mean, the first thing I thought was, this is it, our troubles are over.'

'So,' said West, 'what did you do next?'

'I said I'd take care of the mail, pass it on to her, only I didn't. About a week later, I wrote to the bank, asked them to set up a monthly transfer between the accounts, forged her signature, and that was it. Easy.'

'And you weren't worried you might get found out?' said West. 'You didn't feel guilty about defrauding…?'

'Guilty?' said McKenzie. 'Guilty? Why should I feel guilty? I had nothing, do you understand? Nothing. While she was living the high life, rolling in it, living in a big, fancy house, rent free. Let's face it, she didnae need the money. Look, I just took what I would've got anyway.'

Munro leaned forward and rested his elbows on the

table.

'Tell me, Lorna,' he said, 'I'm curious. Why did you not just transfer the whole lot? Take it all?'

'I'm not that stupid, Inspector,' said McKenzie, 'give me some credit. If I'd have done that it would've aroused suspicion, isn't that the phrase they use? No, see, I figured a small amount every month and no-one would turn a blind eye.'

'I've got to hand it to you, Lorna,' said Munro, sitting back and smiling, 'you certainly thought it through. It's a pity circumstances contrived to trip you up. But, tell me, why on earth didn't you just ask her for the money? I'm sure she would have...'

'Are you mad? Me? Go cap in hand, begging? To her? Do me a favour, that supercilious cow would have been gloating for centuries, using it as an excuse to see me even more. No, that was never an option, believe me.'

'Fair enough,' said Munro, 'so, to return to my earlier question, why did you go back to Dunmore House? See, I think you went to...'

'I told you, I wasn't there, okay? I was not there.'

West gave McKenzie a moment to calm down before speaking.

'Lorna,' she said, 'listen to me. These are very serious allegations being made against you, you're still a young lady, you've got years ahead of you, do you really want to spend them banged up? If you co-operate with us, tell us the truth, it can only work in your favour.'

McKenzie said nothing.

'Your father,' said Munro, 'Callum. I take it he knows nothing of your foray into the world of high finance?'

'That dimwit?' said McKenzie. 'Do me a favour, he's not got the brains for it.'

'He's clever man.'

'Oh, aye? If he's that clever, how come he didnae figure a way out for us years ago? It was there for the taking.'

'Maybe he's just too … honest?' said West.

'Honest? He's not honest, he's just a creep.'

'A creep?' said Munro.

'Aye, a devious, lecherous, creep.'

'What do you mean?'

McKenzie, toying with her hair, glanced up at West and coughed.

'I'd like some water, please.'

West poured her a glass and slid it across the desk.

'Thanks. He used to … when I lived at home, in the caravan … he used to … look at me.'

'Look at you?' said West. 'How? Exactly?'

'Oh, come on, are you that stupid?' said McKenzie. 'Not the way a father should look his daughter. Always leering, like he was thinking stuff.'

'You mean stuff of a sexual nature?'

'Aye.'

'Did he ever … did he ever touch you?' said West.

'No, no, nothing like that,' said McKenzie. 'He just had this habit of … of coming to my room when I was changing or, or entering the bathroom while I was in the shower. His timing was impeccable.'

'But he didn't…'

'No.'

'Because if he did, Lorna,' said West, sympathetically, 'you know we can…'

'There's no need, really. He didn't lay a finger on me.'

'Sounds like you could use a new father,' said Munro.

'Aye, what a present that would be.'

'I'll see what I can do. Now, the thing about these chairs, Lorna, is they're awfully uncomfortable and I cannae take sitting here anymore, so, last chance lassie. Do you want to tell us what you were doing up at Dunmore or …?'

'No comment.'

'Okay, if that's the way you want to play it. Lorna McKenzie, I am charging you with theft, fraud and obtaining goods by deception. Do you understand the charge?'

'Aye.'

'Is there anything you'd like to say in reply to the charge?'

'No.'

'Okay. In that case …'

'What happens now?' said McKenzie.

'You'll return to your cell until your appearance at the Sheriff's Court,' said Munro. 'I hope for your sake they can squeeze us in before the weekend, because I'm not recommending you for bail.'

'Right.'

'And think about that lawyer, lassie. You're going to need…'

Munro, mildly irritated at the interruption, groaned as an audacious knock at the door was followed by the unexpected appearance of an exuberant Constable Reid.

'Chief,' he said, 'am I…?'

'No, no, we're just about done here. What…?'

'Forensics. Freida's place.'

'Anything?'

'No, not yet,' said Reid, 'they're still analysing a few bits and bobs they took from her kitchen, but, did you know they have cameras there?'

'Is that so?' said Munro, casting a sideways glance at McKenzie.

'Aye, all over the place.'

'And?'

'The night in question, they captured a ghostly apparition hovering about the place.'

'A ghost?' said West.

'Aye,' said Reid, 'in a dark red anorak.'

As the severity of the situation finally dawned on her, McKenzie, feeling as vulnerable as a hare in the headlights, looked forlornly up at West.

'Can I … can I ring my Daddy?' she said, pleadingly.

West nodded and smiled compassionately as Munro stood and pushed his chair beneath the table.

'Duncan,' he said, 'would you kindly show our guest back to her room, please.'

'Roger that, chief,' said Reid, 'this way, miss. You've an hour or two before we stop serving supper, breakfast is served in your room between 7am and 9am, light refreshments…'

'Duncan,' said Munro, 'one thing before you go. I met your father earlier, he's a very knowledgeable man.'

'He is that, chief. Hope he didnae chew your ears off.'

'Quite the contrary, but look, when you get home tonight, I think it might be … well, it wouldnae do any harm to stand him a wee drink or two, I think he could use the company.'

'Chief?'

'I've told him about Freida.'

* * *

Campbell returned from the bar, set the drinks down on the table and sat opposite West, grinning like a schoolboy on a first date.

'Bit of a day, eh?' he said, downing half his pint in one go. 'You must be shattered, all that excitement.'

'It's not exciting, Iain,' said West, disparagingly, 'getting married, that's exciting. Watching a thunderstorm over the Sierra Nevada, that's exciting. This job is more like finishing The Times crossword; the only thing you get at the end of it is a sense of relief.'

'Aye, okay,' said Campbell, 'but even so, it is interesting; you must enjoy it.'

'Yeah, yeah I suppose I do.'

'Can't be easy, though, having to work with…'

West regarded him suspiciously as his words tailed off.

'Go on,' she said.

'Och, no, you're alright.'

'No, I want to hear it, can't be easy working with…?'

'The chief. Inspector Munro.'

'How do you mean?' said West.

'Well,' said Campbell, staring into his beer, 'he can be a bit harsh. Cutting, you know?'

'Ah, did he hurt your feelings?' said West, giggling. 'Do you need a hug?'

'Oh, very funny, you've not been on the receiving end.'

'Trust me, Iain, I've taken more put-downs and sarcastic asides than you'll ever get, and you know what? It did me good. Don't be such a softy, it's just banter, take it with a pinch of salt.'

'I know, but he made me feel this big,' said Campbell, 'I mean, the way he embarrassed me when I called you in the car and later, when he lost his rag, treating me like I'm some kind of numpty.'

'Oh, grow up Iain, for God's sake,' said West, her hackles rising, 'you're a bloody police sergeant, you know how it is.'

'Aye, I do, but it's not just that, it's the way he takes the piss, about me … about me liking you.'

'He's just looking out for me, that's all. Forget about it.'

'I can't, it's not right, it's demeaning. I was thinking, maybe, maybe you should have a word.'

'What did you say?' said West, enraged. 'You want me to ask a D.I. to back off because you're a bit sensitive? Fight your own battles, mate, I'm not here to…'

'Aye, alright, alright,' said Campbell, 'I'm sorry. I just… look, let's change the subject, okay? So, will we have another drink before we eat? I quite fancy…'

West drained her glass, pulled her bag over her shoulder and stood up.

'Actually, Iain, you know what?' she said, 'I'm not that hungry anymore. I'll see you tomorrow.'

* * *

Restricted, as he was, by his two-fingered typing

technique, the charge sheet had taken longer to complete than anticipated. Munro sighed wearily, switched off the desk lamp and groaned as the clatter of heels behind him resounded off the wooden floor.

'Isobel,' he said, without turning around, 'I've been expecting you.'

'I'm flattered,' said Crawford, whimsically.

'I assume you're here because Nick telephoned you?'

'He did, he said...'

'I can guess what he said.'

'So,' said Crawford, purring like a kitten on the prowl, 'I thought, maybe, we could...'

'Listen, Isobel,' said Munro, tersely, 'I'm not being funny, but Nick, in his caffeine-induced state of frenzy, has jumped the gun.'

'Oh?'

'He had no right to call you.'

'I see,' said Crawford. 'So, when he said you had it all wrapped up...'

'I'll wrap him up,' said Munro. 'Look, the fact of the matter is we're far from done here. We are holding someone and she's been charged. But with fraud, not murder.'

'How irritating. Want to fill me in?'

'Soon, Isobel, soon,' said Munro, 'but not just now, you'll get the report tomorrow. Now, I really do need to get some rest. I'm sorry, sorry that you've had a wasted journey.'

'Not wasted, James,' said Crawford, 'just not as fulfilling as I'd hoped. Come on, I'll walk you to your car.'

Munro, unaccustomed to being the hunted, especially when the predator was of a female persuasion, hastily jumped in his car, lowered the window and turned the ignition.

'We will have that drink, Isobel, I promise,' he said, apologetically, as the starter motor whined, 'just as soon as...'

He flipped the ignition, tried again and cursed under his breath as the only response was a sound resembling the last, dying gasps of some hapless creature slipping the mortal coil.

'The engine,' said Crawford, 'it's not turning over.'

Munro regarded her with a look of contempt.

'You should get a job with traffic, Isobel,' he said, 'your talents are wasted behind a desk.'

'Come on, I'll give you a lift.'

'No, no, you're alright, I'll get a…'

'Stop being so bloody stubborn. Move.'

* * *

Munro buckled up and adjusted the vanity mirror on the visor to get a clear view through the rear window.

'Let me know what's on the meter when we get there,' he said, 'I'll settle up tomorrow.'

Crawford allowed herself a wry grin.

'You need to relax a bit, James,' she said, 'it would do you the world of good.'

'How can I relax, Isobel? You gave me five days to crack this and we've barely enough time left to crack an egg, let alone a murder.'

'So, you're no nearer to finding out who…'

'Actually, I am.'

'But your suspect isn't the girl you're holding?'

'No. Poor, wee lassie, I cannae blame her for taking the money, but I don't think...'

Munro tapped Crawford on the arm.

'Slow down,' he said, pointing through the windscreen at a middle-aged couple locked in a loving embrace outside The Oak Bar, 'isn't that…?'

'My God, it is. It's Nick!' said Crawford. 'Well, bugger me, I wonder who she is?'

'If I'm not mistaken,' said Munro, 'I believe *that* is Mr. MacDonald from the yacht club.'

Chapter 15

Munro joined West at the breakfast table, her plate piled high with square sausage, black pudding, extra bacon, one fried tomato, two tattie scones and a runny egg.

'This,' she said, stuffing her cheeks as though she'd not eaten for a week, 'is what makes this job worthwhile.'

'Where's your porage?' said Munro.

'If I wanted a bowl of gruel,' said West, 'I'd get a part in Oliver Twist.'

Munro smiled.

'Okay, by the by, we've no car this morning, so we'll have to get a taxi.'

West, grinning, sat back and downed her cutlery.

'So, someone stay out last night then?' she said.

'No, no,' said Munro, 'it's at the station, broken down. I've telephoned young Duncan and asked him to arrange a mechanic.'

'So, how'd you get back? Did you take the bus?'

'That was my intention, but I was forced to accept a lift instead.'

'Isobel?'

'Aye, Isobel, that woman will not take no for an answer, and, if you must know, it was just a lift, no drinks and definitely no supper. Which reminds me, I thought you were stepping out with Sergeant Campbell last night, did you enjoy yourself?'

'No,' said West, 'early night.'

'I see, well, I'll not pry, just as long as you're okay, not upset or anything.'

'No, not upset, thanks for asking. Let's just say that under that burly exterior, is a very immature ... so, what're we doing first?'

'Well, once we've got ourselves some transport, we're away to see Inverkip's very own Mr. Personality of the Year.'

* * *

Munro was content with his ageing Peugeot Estate. It was comfortable, lived-in, a little frayed around the edges and, unlike the squad car he'd unofficially hijacked from the pool, it provided a degree of anonymity.

'Shall we have the sirens?' said West as she eagerly slipped in to the driver's seat.

'No Charlie,' said Munro, 'we shall not. Travelling in a glorified ice-cream van, we're conspicuous enough as it is. We don't need to draw any more attention to ourselves.'

* * *

Rudy Kappelhoff downed tools as the squad car pulled up outside his shop, opened the door and, for the first time since they'd met, smiled. He wiped his hands on his apron and welcomed them inside.

'Mr. Kappelhoff,' said Munro, 'I hope we're not disturbing you.'

'No, whatever I am doing can wait. Come, we will sit in my room, it is more pleasant.'

West shrugged her shoulders in disbelief as they followed him through to the back.

'I will make you tea or coffee, or a glass of milk, if you like?'

'No, thank you,' said West, 'very kind, but I'm fine.'

'Inspector?'

'No, thanks all the same,' said Munro, frowning, 'but if you don't mind me saying so, Mr. Kappelhoff, you seem a little … subdued, not your usual, ebullient, self. Are you sleeping alright?'

Kappelhoff sat down and smiled.

'I am sleeping very well, Inspector,' he said. 'You want to know why? Because the anger has gone. Whatever my Freida did in the past, whatever reasons she had for leaving, she has made up for it now. She has taken my anger with her.'

'And do you know why you feel so much better, Rudy?' said West excitedly, as though addressing a nine-year old. 'I'll tell you, it's because you've purged yourself of all that negative energy. And now that you radiate positivity, people will be drawn to you, you'll be surrounded by love, light and happiness, in abundance.'

'Good grief,' said Munro.

'Yes,' said Kappelhoff, 'I agree. Good grief. So, you are not here for a social visit, tell me what I can do to help.'

'It's the other way round, actually,' said Munro, 'we've some news for you, a surprise, of sorts. I'm just hoping it's a pleasant one.'

'Good,' said Kappelhoff, smiling softly, 'I very much like surprises.'

Munro pulled up a chair, folded his arms and, with a scratch of the nose, addressed Kappelhoff in a tone normally reserved for the recently widowed.

'Did you, er, did you know Freida was pregnant when she left you?' he said.

Kappelhoff stopped smiling.

'You are crazy man,' he said, 'how could she be?'

'Well …'

'Doctors told us for many years, it is not possible for her to have child.'

'Why was that?' said West. 'Was she infertile?'

'No, lady, not her, me. The doctors are saying my, my

sperms, they not swim so good. So, it was other man's baby, yes? And that is why she left?'

'No,' said Munro, 'it appears not. You see, during the course of our investigation, we have, purely by chance, found a match between your DNA and that of a young lady. You'll be pleased to know there's nothing wrong with your, er, sperms Mr. Kappelhoff. You have a daughter. Her name's Lorna.'

Kappelhoff glanced at West, then at Munro, his eyes misting over.

'And you are sure?' he said. 'This is not some kind of joke to…'

'100% sure,' said West. 'No doubt about it.'

'I will kill that doctor.'

'So, the question is, would you like to meet her?'

'Would I…? Of course,' said Kappelhoff, beaming, 'of course I wish to meet her, I…'

'Good, but hold on,' said Munro, 'don't get too excited, not just yet. See, first of all, we have to ask her if she wants to meet you, if she does, then fine, but if she doesn't, then, I'm afraid, we cannot introduce you; it's something you'll have to try and arrange for yourself, do you understand?'

'Yes, okay, I think so, but why would she not…'

'It could be a bit of a shock for her, Mr. Kappelhoff,' said West, 'I mean, finding out that the man who raised you is not your father, it's a lot to take in. You might have to give her some time to come to terms with the fact.'

'Of course, okay.'

'And there's something else,' said Munro, 'which, I'm afraid, won't make things any easier. You see, Lorna has been arrested and charged with fraud. We're holding her in custody until we get a date with the Sheriff's Court.'

'Fraud?' said Kappelhoff. 'That is like stealing, yes?'

'Yes. And it's very serious. Chances are, she'll be going to jail for a wee while.'

'That is too bad,' said Kappelhoff, despondently, 'but,

I will visit every day, and when she is released, we will…'

'Good,' said West, 'in that case, we'll give you a call just as soon as we've spoken with Lorna. Let you know what she says.'

* * *

The short hop back to Gourock along the deserted, coastal road filled West with an overwhelming urge to hit the lights and floor the accelerator.

'This is a perfect stretch,' she said, glancing at Munro, 'there's no-one around, just a short blast, what do you say?'

'No,' said Munro.

'Just for a second.'

'No.'

'I'll ease off when we hit sixty.'

'Charlie,' said Munro, candidly, 'unless we have just cause, or you can show me a piece of paper proving you've achieved Class 1 status behind the wheel, I'll thank you to respect the speed limit. Okay?'

'Spoilsport,' said West. 'Bet if I was a bloke, you'd … what's up? You've got that look on your face.'

Munro hesitated as he gathered his words.

'Do you remember yesterday,' he said, 'Nick…'

'You mean, majorly hungover?'

'Aye. We saw him last night, on the Inverkip Road, outside a bar.'

'Hair of the dog, I expect. Kill or cure.'

'He was with a young, I mean, he was with a lady friend, canoodling outside.'

'What of it?' said West. 'It's not a crime to…'

'I know, I know,' said Munro, 'but something's niggling me. I mean, why would he say he got blootered with someone who doesnae drink? Why not just say he was out with a friend and had one too many?'

'Dunno. Maybe she's married.'

'Aye, there is that, of course, but…'

'I can guess what's coming,' said West, 'go on, what do you want?'

'Well, if you're agreeable, I'm not forcing you, mind, I'd like you to drop in the bar this evening, casual like, and ask for Nick by name, see if they know him.'

'Then what?'

'I'm not really sure. We'll play it by ear.'

'You do know spying on a fellow police officer can lead to…'

'Who said anything about spying? Just enquiring after a friend called…'

'Yeah, right, like there's bound to be another Nick…'

'Do you know how many folk there are in Dumfries alone that go by the name of James Munro?'

'Dozens, I expect.'

'Well, there you go then.'

* * *

The mechanic, a stocky individual whose rear end was testing the build quality of his overalls to the limit, was buried beneath the bonnet of Munro's car outside the station, cussing as he fiddled with a component. West parked alongside and killed the engine.

'Hello there,' said Munro, delighted at the prospect of having it fixed, 'I understand the distributor failed, have you managed to sort it?'

The mechanic grunted as he eased himself upright, turned to face Munro and scowled, his shaven head glistening with tiny beads of sweat.

'Is this your vehicle?' he said, accusingly, as he waved a screwdriver.

'Aye, one hundred and twenty thousand miles, full service history and still going strong.'

'Have you not considered buying something a little more … modern? Something that doesnae need a starting handle to get it going?'

'Very droll,' said Munro, 'I'll have you know this automobile has covered most of the British Isles, and in forty odd years, she's never complained, not once. Unlike yourself.'

'Tomorrow,' said the mechanic, brusquely, 'if you're lucky, mind.'

* * *

Munro, drawn by the commotion from beyond the front door, dashed inside to find a stressed Constable Reid on the wrong side of the reception desk, doing his utmost to calm an extremely irate and somewhat volatile visitor.

'I'll not tell you again, sir,' he said, 'if you refuse to calm down, I shall be forced to...'

'What the hell is going on?' said Munro.

'This gentleman, chief, he's being a wee bit ... obstreperous; keeps insisting on...'

'Aye, that's right!' said Callum McKenzie. 'I insist on seeing my daughter, she telephoned me last night, I've every right to...'

West, intervening, leapt forward and stood so close that McKenzie could feel her breath on his face.

'Oi!' she yelled, through gritted teeth. 'Back off, sit down and shut up, or I'll do you for threatening behaviour, got it?'

McKenzie, taken aback by the ferocity of her negotiating skills, duly complied.

'Good,' said Munro, 'perhaps now we can enjoy an air of civility about the place, surround ourselves with some peace, love and understanding, okay?'

West, grinning as she struggled to suppress her laughter, whipped round reception and headed for her desk.

'It's all a bit quiet here, Duncan,' she said, 'where's Sergeant Campbell?'

'Wheelie bin fire, miss, down by the bookies, he'll not be long.'

'And Inspector McGreevy?' said Munro.

'Stuck in traffic, chief.'

'Traffic? His house is less than...'

'Aye,' said Constable Reid, 'I know, figure he must be on a shout, you know?'

McKenzie stood and took a few tentative steps towards Munro.

'Inspector,' he said, quietly, 'sorry, look, I didnae mean to kick off like that, it's just that Lorna said…'

'All in good time, Mr. McKenzie,' said Munro, 'please sit and wait until you're called, I have some urgent business to attend to first.'

'Right, and I suppose it's more important than…'

'Aye, as matter of fact, Mr. McKenzie, it is. I have to attend to a package that's arrived all the way from the Indian sub-continent.'

'Oh. Okay.'

Munro slung his jacket over the back of his chair and sat with a sigh.

'Charlie,' he said, 'stick the kettle on, there's a box of Darjeeling by the sink, I'm positively parched. Oh, and tell Duncan to take our visitor to the interview room, we'll be along shortly.'

* * *

McKenzie, hands in pockets, paced the floor like a lifer in solitary, counting every step, toe to heel, wall to wall, muttering under his breath as his frustration grew.

'At last,' he said, as Munro entered the room, 'I've been waiting for…'

'Have a seat, Mr. McKenzie.'

'I'd rather…'

'Sit!' said West.

McKenzie promptly obeyed and sat like a chastised child, knees together, his hands folded in his lap.

'So,' he said, not daring to look at West, 'when can I…?'

'When we say so,' said Munro, 'first you need to understand why Lorna is here. Now, when you spoke to her last night, did she tell you why she was being held?'

'No, not really, just said she'd been accused of theft. Has she robbed someone?'

'Aye, she has,' said Munro, 'Freida.'

'Freida?' said McKenzie, genuinely surprised. 'But ... but how? I mean...?'

'All that correspondence from the bank she said she was forwarding? She wasn't. She used the information to gain access to Freida's accounts. She's been charged with fraud and deception and, before you get your hopes up, there is absolutely every chance she will be going to jail.'

'But I don't ... her own mother?' said McKenzie. 'Dear God, what on earth was she ... why? I mean, she had a good job, she didn't have to...'

'No, she didn't,' said West, 'she didn't have a job at all. She didn't work at the Co-Op and she certainly wasn't Assistant Manager.'

'Are you joking me?' said McKenzie. 'She told me she...'

'What she said, and what she did, are two different things. She's been staying in a squalid little flat in Paisley, claiming welfare and living off Freida's money.'

'I don't believe it, I just don't ... wait till I see her, I'll give her a piece of my mind, no daughter of mine is going to...'

'Mr. McKenzie,' said Munro, sternly, 'there's something else you need to know.'

Munro paused momentarily.

'Charlie,' he said, 'would you pop along and see Lorna now. Fill her in about everything first...'

'You mean...?'

'Aye, then ask if she still wants to see her father.'

Munro waited until West had left the room before continuing.

'See here, Callum,' said Munro, lowering his voice, 'this is a wee bit awkward for the both of us, so, all I can say is, brace yourself for a bit of a revelation.'

'A revelation?' said McKenzie. 'What kind of revelation?'

'During the course of our investigation, we've cross-matched DNA samples taken from everyone we've interviewed who may, or may not, have been involved in Freida's death.'

'So?'

'It's thrown up some bad news. For you.'

McKenzie took a deep breath and swallowed hard.

'What kind of bad news?' he said, quietly.

'Lorna, is not your daughter.'

McKenzie sat, stony-faced, staring at Munro, until, unexpectedly, he broke a smile and began to laugh, nervously.

'That is ridiculous,' he said, 'that is the most ridiculous thing I've ever…'

'Freida was already pregnant when you moved in together,' said Munro, 'she was carrying her husband's child.'

West returned, glanced at Munro from behind the door and nodded.

'Okay Charlie, bring her in.'

Lorna took the chair next to Munro, sat quietly and stared at her father, her face devoid of expression. McKenzie smiled back, tight-lipped and shook his head.

'Lorna,' he said softly, before erupting in a furious rage, 'what the hell are you playing at lassie?' he yelled. 'Lying about the job? Lying about…!'

'Mr. McKenzie!' said West, 'you'll conduct yourself in a civilised manner or not at all! Do I make myself clear?'

McKenzie slumped back in his seat red-faced as Lorna looked on, dispassionately.

'Sorry,' he said, trying to compose himself, 'Lorna, hen, tell me, what's all this about the job?'

'What's it to you?'

'And the theft? I mean, your own mother? Why did…'

'None of your business.'

'If you needed money, why didn't you just ask? I'd have done something, anything…'

Lorna stared blankly into his eyes and huffed with

indifference.

'So, that's it?' said McKenzie, 'that's all you've got to say for yourself?'

'I'm ashamed,' she said.

'Aye, so you should be. It's a terrible thing you've…'

'I'm ashamed of you.'

'What?'

'You're not fit to be a father.'

'How dare you!' said McKenzie. 'Who the hell do you think you're talking to?'

'See, I know what you did, Daddy. I know why you stopped being a teacher…'

'What? That's not true, that was just a … just a … misunderstanding, nothing was proved.'

'And when you couldn't find any more schoolgirls, you turned to me, spying on me naked, getting your perverted kicks…'

'Are you serious?'

'Aye, too right I am. I've never been more bloody serious in my entire life. You want to know why I lied about the job? Why I robbed Mammy's bank? So's I'd never have to see you again. Never have to share a house with you again. Never have to breathe the same air as you again. You're a filthy, twisted pervert, and you know what? I'm glad you're not my father. I'm sick of the sight of you.'

McKenzie, dejected, rose slowly to his feet and shuffled towards the door.

'I'll take you out,' said Munro, 'follow me.'

'Can I go back to my cell now Sergeant?' said Lorna, smiling with relief, 'and would you do me a wee favour? Would you tell Mr. Kappelhoff I'd be delighted to meet him?'

* * *

Munro stood on the steps outside the station and couldn't help but feel a pang of sympathy for McKenzie as he watched him amble, dejected, along the street; his scuffed, yellow coat, flapping in the breeze.

'What's up with him?' said Sergeant Campbell, appearing by his side.

'Och, he's just had some bad news, that's all. How about you, Iain? Good day, so far?'

'No chief,' said Campbell, 'mind numbingly dull. Just back from reprimanding a bunch of neds conducting a scientific experiment.'

'Oh?'

'Using a wheelie bin as a combustion chamber and a bottle of petroleum as the accelerant. Had to run them back to their parents.'

'You're not charging them with anything?' said Munro. 'Criminal damage?'

'No chief, it's not worth it,' said Campbell, 'too much paperwork, besides they'll probably get a good hiding off the big fella when he finds out.'

'Never did me any harm,' said Munro, 'I must say, Iain, I'm not keen on all this politically correct rubbish being bandied about these days, if you ask me, it's gone too far.'

'I'm with you on that, chief,' said Campbell. 'Listen, I don't suppose…'

'Interview room. Give her a moment to get young Lorna back in her cell.'

'Right, thanks.'

'Incidentally Iain, have you seen Nick about the place today?'

'No.'

'And no-one's called him?'

'Aye, Duncan, a couple of times, but he's not picking up.'

'Do you think he's alright?' said Munro. 'Should we not nip round and…'

'Och, he'll be fine, chief, why not give him a call yourself, if it makes you feel better.'

'I will that, Iain. I will that.'

Munro's eyes flickered with a glint of optimistic

delight as he noticed his car standing locked and unattended. He muttered under his breath, apologising to nobody in particular for berating the mechanic, slipped nimbly behind the wheel, placed the key in the ignition, leant back, closed his eyes, and gave it a twist.

'Bugger,' he said, pulling the phone from his pocket and dialling McGreevy.

'James, you okay?'

'Nick,' said Munro, 'I'm surprised you've answered, young Duncan's been trying to reach you all day. Are you not answering your calls?'

'Sorry,' said McGreevy, 'been a bit tied up…'

'The lads were getting a wee bit anxious, that's all, not knowing…'

'Och, for crying out loud,' said McGreevy, 'I told Constable Shaw last night, he was on lates. Change to the duty roster, I left it with him.'

'Okay, well, no harm done. As long you're safe.'

'It's all good, James, just a few unexpected chores to deal with on the domestic front, you understand?'

'Aye, okay, I'll tell the lads, put their minds at rest. Oh, and Nick, give my best to Mr. MacDonald, won't you?'

Chapter 16

There was little about The Oak Bar that looked inviting. A converted stable-block set back from the main road, its blackened windows, faded signs and neglected flower troughs filled with wilting plants did little to suggest a warm welcome and convivial atmosphere awaited those who dared to pass through its portals. Munro, lamenting the loss of his unobtrusive Peugeot, sped by, killed the lights, and parked the patrol car on the grass verge, fifty yards down the road.

'Now, don't go overboard, Charlie,' he said, 'we don't want to raise any eyebrows, understand?'

'Feel like I should be wearing a wire,' said West, jokingly, 'leave it to me.'

* * *

The frosty reception she'd half expected, did not materialise. There were no withering looks, no icy stares and no demands to leave, in fact, not a single soul took a blind bit of notice as she sauntered up to the bar. Two men perched on stools were sipping whisky, looking for winners in the racing pages of the Daily Record, whilst a young couple, engrossed in their phones, sat silently opposite each other at a corner table, looking, to all intents and purposes, like strangers in a waiting room. The sound of lilting fiddles wafted from the speakers on the wall as the barman, clean cut in an open-necked shirt, greeted her with a warm smile and a roguish glint in his eye.

'Alright, hen?' he said. 'What can I get you?'

'Vodka and tonic, please,' said West, 'no ice. Quiet in here, isn't it?'

'Aye, best make the most of it, it'll be heaving in an hour. Will I make that a large one?'

'No, thanks, haven't got long,' said West, 'someone said Nick might be here?'

'Nick?' said the barman, frowning inquisitively as he set down her drink.

'Yeah, we're mates from way back, I'm only up for a few days, thought I'd give him a shout.'

'Oh, okay. He was in last night, got blootered, but that's between you and me, okay?'

'Sounds like Nick,' said West, 'don't suppose you know where he is now?'

'No, but Maureen might...'

'Maureen?'

'Aye, he and she, they've a wee thing going, I'll give her a shout, hold on.'

West sipped her drink as she surveyed the pub, copper pots and pans, and the odd, dusty sprig of dried heather, hung from the ceiling; the walls were crammed with reproduction prints of snowy, highland scenes, and a framed certificate behind the bar read "Maureen Connolly. Licensed to sell Beers, Wine and Spirits for consumption on or off the premises".

A dour looking woman squeezed past the barman and approached West as though she were squaring up for a fight. Average height, average build, too much lipstick, bottle-blonde hair and a face carved from stone.

'What do you want?' she said, her eyes narrowing.

'You must be Maureen,' said West, smiling.

'Doesnae matter who I am. I said, what do you want?'

'The barman said you might know where I can find Nick.'

'Nick who?'

West paused and, with a subtle shake of the head, smirked and finished her drink.

'If you don't know,' she said, 'then I'm obviously wasting my time.'

'Who are you?' said Connolly.

'Just a friend. An old friend. Up from London.'

Connolly stepped forward and leaned in to West.

'See here, hen, Nick doesnae have any friends. He doesnae need any friends, ken what I'm saying?'

'You know what?' said West, zipping her coat. 'It doesn't matter, I'll ask someone else, thanks for your…'

'You listen to me,' said Connolly, 'you leave him be, or you'll be on your way to the infirmary before you know it, understand?'

'Yeah, yeah,' said West, 'look at me, I'm shaking. See you round.'

* * *

West cut a lonely figure as Munro, lights off, reversed slowly up the street to meet her.

'Okay?' he said as she jumped on board.

'Yeah, I think so,' said West, pensively.

'What is it, Charlie? Did something happen?'

'No, nothing, it's all just a bit, odd. I've just been threatened with a trip to the hospital.'

'What?' said Munro, appalled. 'Who was he? Would you recognise him if…?'

'Not he, she. The landlady.'

'The landlady? What did she say?'

'Well, basically, stop looking for Nick.'

'Is that so? What did she look like?'

'Average,' said West, 'jeans a size too small, dyed, blonde hair and a face like Medusa.'

'That's her!' said Munro excitedly, 'Charlie, that's the lady I saw with Nick.'

'Well, there's something odd going on, I mean, the barman was fine, he knew Nick and he was more than happy to talk to me about him, but she, she was, I don't know, not over-protective exactly, or ... or jealous, like some girlfriends might be. She was more like a ... like a raving nutter.'

'Okay, look, I know it might seem like we're taking our eyes off the prize here, but something's not right. We need to find out what her name is. What are you grinning at?'

* * *

Munro stopped the car, flicked on the hazards and called the station.

'Duncan, you've not left yet?' he said.

'On my way now, chief,' said Constable Reid, 'did you want something?'

'Aye, listen,' said Munro, 'I've a wee mission for you.'

'A mission? Brilliant! What is it?'

'I need a background check, but listen Duncan, this is very sensitive, you cannae breathe a word of this to anyone, do you understand?'

'Roger that.'

'And you cannae use the computer in the office.'

'Nae bother, so long as you don't need me to access official files, I can use my computer at home.'

'Good. Maureen Connolly. She owns The Oak Bar...'

'I know that place,' said Constable Reid, 'never been in, looks a right dump.'

'Find out whatever you can, okay? And let me know as soon as you have anything, anything at all.'

'Roger that, chief. I'm on it.'

* * *

Munro heaved a troubled sigh as he parked up outside the station and killed the engine.

'What's up?' said West. 'You look done in.'

'Och, I'm okay Charlie. I can't help but think this is all going to get a wee bit messy, that's all. And that fellow with a head like a potato dawdling over my car doesnae help.'

'That's why God gave us taxis,' said West.

'He did that,' said Munro, 'shame he didn't equip them with drivers who didn't need a sat-nav to get from A to B. Incidentally, how's young Lorna doing? Is she okay?'

'Yeah, I think so. She said she'd like to meet Kappelhoff.'

'Good,' said Munro, 'so, you think she's okay then, mentally I mean, not too ... fragile?'

'No, not at all, why?'

'We need to question her again. I need to know what she was doing at Dunmore. She knows more than she's letting on.'

'But we've charged her,' said West, 'you know you can't question her anymore, it's not...'

'Och, Charlie, I know that, that's why I'm not going to question her about the theft,' said Munro, 'I'm going to question her on suspicion of murder.'

'What? You really think...'

'No, I don't think she's capable, but the fact is she hardly flinched when we told her that her mother had died, and we have her on CCTV at Dunmore around the time of Freida's death. Trust me Charlie, she's the one who stashed that envelope beneath the mattress, and she knows who killed Freida.'

'Well, on that happy note, I'd say it's about time we had some dinner.'

'We?' said Munro, mildly surprised. 'Is Dirty Harry not taking you out tonight?'

'Very funny. No, he is not.'

'Not fallen out, I hope,' said Munro.

'No,' said West, 'he's alright, just a bit too, I don't know, tough on the outside but...'

'Aye, I know the type, like a blancmange in battledress.'

'Yes,' said West, giggling, 'that sounds about right,

anyway, I'm not going to lead him on, wouldn't be fair.'

'That's very noble of you, Charlie, very noble indeed, but a shame, nonetheless. It means I'll have to return the morning suit. Still, I'm sure you'll have no shortage of suitors now.'

'Really?' said West. 'How'd you figure that out?'

'Why, you're radiating positivity, Charlie, you have love and light in abundance.'

* * *

Munro, an ardent fan of literary classics, had, in the past, joyfully devoured such masterpieces as *The Pilgrim's Progress*, *Don Quixote* and *The Grapes of Wrath*, but, tucked comfortably beneath the sheets, his pyjamas buttoned to the neck, he yawned uncontrollably as he struggled to pass page 97 of *Finnegan's Wake*.

'Utter rubbish,' he said, tossing it to one side as he answered his phone.

'Chief,' said Constable Reid, 'are you okay to talk?'

'Fire away, Duncan.'

'Okay, Maureen Connolly, nothing on social media so I had to do some digging round the council records, stuff like that, and it's all looking a wee bit, well, incestuous.'

'What do you mean?'

'Get this,' said Reid, 'Maureen Connolly used to live and work at Dunmore House.'

'Dunmore House? Are you sure?' said Munro.

'Positive, so I asked my Daddy if he remembered her, subtle like, I didnae go into detail.'

'And?'

'Strangest thing, he said "vaguely", and took himself off to the garage.'

'At this time of night?' said Munro.

'Aye, I think he's losing it,' said Reid, 'so anyway, I gave Mrs. Fraser a wee tinkle, I mean, if anyone would've known her, she would.'

'And did she?'

'Too right. According to Mrs. Fraser, Connolly got

the heave-ho not long after my Daddy was sacked, she said there was some kind of altercation between her, Freida Kappelhoff and the lady of the house, and it got so out of hand, they had to call the police.'

'Dear, dear,' said Munro, 'and they seem so respectable, too.'

'That's not all,' said Reid, 'she said the officer who handled the case was some kind of dreamboat, they were all falling for him. A Sergeant McGreevy.'

Munro threw his head back and sighed.

'Thanks Duncan,' he said, 'excellent job, but not a word, mind, not a word to anyone. Understand?'

'Roger that, chief. My lips are sealed.'

Chapter 17

A force 7 westerly, powering in from the Atlantic, brought with it torrential rain, a roaring trade in sales of worthless umbrellas and the likelihood of the regatta being postponed until the inclement weather abated.

McGreevy, cursing at the prospect of having to cancel and then re-instigate temporary road closures, pored over the duty roster for the coming week as the wind threatened to rip the slates off the roof. He cocked an ear at the rumpus in reception.

'Duncan,' said Munro as he helped West out of her sopping coat, 'I cannae go on like this, I need you to call King Edward and tell that blethering idiot that if I don't get my car today, I will arrest him on suspicion of malingering, have you got that?'

'Aye, Roger that, chief,' said Reid, 'and before I forget, Miss McKenzie's appearance in court – it's set for Monday, 9 am.'

'Okay, best tell her we're obliged to extend our hospitality for the duration of the weekend; see if she needs anything, a change of clothes perhaps.'

Munro glanced up as McGreevy, hands in pockets, strolled casually from his office.

'Nick, my but you're early,' he said, mildly surprised, 'have you some worms to catch?'

'Actually, no, James, I'm working on a Plan B just in case this God-awful weather doesnae blow over soon.'

'Och, it's a few drops of rain, if you're not used to it by now, you should consider moving south.'

'Maybe I will, James. Tea? Looks like you could both use a brew.'

'Very kind, I'm sure,' said Munro. 'No Iain this morning?'

'No, he's gone to inspect some wind damage at the golf club.'

'So, there's no spare car?'

'Doubt it, why? Do you have calls to make?'

'Aye, and that mechanic has left me stranded.'

McGreevy winked, pulled his hand from his pocket and tossed Munro a key.

'Here,' he said, 'take mine. I'll not need it till this afternoon, so long as I can have it back by 2pm, it's all yours.'

'Much obliged,' said Munro, taken aback by his act of spontaneous generosity.

'So, where're we at, James?' said McGreevy. 'Are we any closer to wrapping this mess up?'

'Aye, we're getting there, we're waiting on a few more results from forensics, they're running some more detailed tests on a couple of…'

'Okay. I see the McKenzie girl's still here, have you not charged her yet?'

'We have.'

'But not with Freida's death?'

'No, of course not; we've no proof, there's no evidence to suggest…'

McGreevy turned for his office, beckoned Munro to follow and gently closed the door.

'Lean on her, James,' he said angrily, under his breath, 'push her a wee bit, it won't take much to make her crack, then we can put this to bed.'

Munro, stupefied by the proposition, watched as McGreevy returned to his chair and aimlessly shuffled the papers on his desk.

'That may be a technique you're used to employing, Nick,' he said, 'but just for the record, I'll not lean on anyone, anyone at all, unless I think they're guilty. Got that?'

'Och, James, for Christ's sake, I'm only trying to speed things along. Look, from where I'm sitting, that wee lassie's guilty as hell, she's traumatised, I mean, finding out her father was playing the field with schoolgirls, it's bound to have affected her. She's unhinged. Maybe you should get a shrink in, have them do a psychiatric assessment, at least then we'll know why she took it out on her mother.'

'No,' said Munro, bluntly, 'I'll do nothing of the kind, and to be perfectly honest, Nick, I'm surprised and somewhat disappointed that you could even make such a suggestion.'

McGreevy, silently fuming, ran a finger around the collar of his shirt and faced Munro.

'James,' he said, lowering his voice, 'see here. In a day or two, this place will be rammed to the gills, over-run with folk paying top dollar to watch a few boats bobbing about on the water, spending their hard-earned cash in the hotels, and the bars, and the restaurants. Now, I asked you up here because I thought you could sort this out for me, if...'

'If you're not happy, Nick,' said Munro, reaching for the door, 'I'll have a wee word with Isobel, I'm sure she'll be only too happy for the lads in C.I.D. to take over.'

McGreevy stood, turned his back on Munro and stared from the window at the deluge cascading down the street outside.

'That won't be necessary,' he said, scratching the back of his bristling, close-cropped head, 'just do what you can. Incidentally, I don't suppose you've noticed a place called

The Oak Bar on your travels, have you?'

'I have, and I've seen crematoriums with more appeal than that excuse for a tavern.'

'So, you've not been in for a wee bevy then? You and Charlie, perhaps?'

'I'm not in the habit of frequenting bars, Nick. Not my cup of tea. Not my cup of tea, at all.'

* * *

'What's up?' said West as she followed Munro down to the cells. 'You look like you've swallowed a wasp.'

Munro paused on the steps, glanced over his shoulder and spoke quietly.

'You know when you're on a walk up a hill and a tiny, insignificant, wee stone gets in your boot and makes your life a misery?' he said.

'Yeah, been there.'

'Well, this one's called McGreevy. And it's causing me a great deal of discomfort. Listen, not a word about last night, the bar, okay? Or anything else for that matter, if he asks, you tell him nothing, understood?'

'Got ya,' said West, 'and by the way, how come we're not using the interview room?'

'Oh, I think she'll be more at ease in the comfort of her own room, don't you? A little less … defensive.'

* * *

McKenzie was sitting on the bunk, her knees pulled to her chest. A thin, blue blanket hung loosely around her shoulders, her nose buried deep in a paperback.

'Hello Lorna,' said West, 'mind if we join you?'

McKenzie seemed unusually content, her face a picture of serenity.

'Aye, the more the merrier,' she said, softly. 'Do you know something? I'd forgotten just how much I enjoy reading, I cannae remember the last time I picked up a book.'

'Och, you're a girl after my own heart, lassie,' said Munro. 'You know, you can lose yourself in a book, but you can find yourself, too.'

McKenzie frowned as she digested his words.

'That's very profound,' she said, 'you're quite clever, aren't you?'

'No, no,' said Munro, 'I just think a little … differently … to other folk, that's all. By the by, Lorna, I don't recall you having a book when…'

'No, I didn't, it was that nice, wee Constable upstairs, he lent it me.'

'Constable Reid?' said West. 'That was kind of him.'

'Aye, he's lovely,' said McKenzie.

'And how's he been treating you?' said Munro. 'Any complaints about room service?'

'Not with him at my beck and call. Anyway, what's up? You here for a wee chat or something?'

'Yes, we are,' said West, 'unofficially.'

Munro leaned forward, elbows resting on his thighs, his hands clasped together. He smiled, a half smile, as though deliberating over a menu, and locked eyes with McKenzie. To her surprise, the hard, ice-blue gaze which had previously filled her with dread, was now as warm and inviting as the Mediterranean.

'See Lorna,' he said softly, his voice as soothing as a lullaby to an infant's ears, 'we're in a wee bit of a pickle here. You'll not be with us much longer, and, in a day or two, Charlie here and myself will be off to pastures new. Now, the last thing I want to do, is to leave you in the hands of someone who doesnae give a damn if you live or die. Do you understand what I'm saying?'

'Aye,' said McKenzie, 'I think so.'

'Good. Okay, we need to make some headway, so, once more, off the record, what were you doing at your mother's apartment on the night she died?'

McKenzie's eyes flitted to West and glazed over.

'I can't,' she said.

'Lorna, listen to me,' said Munro, 'once we're gone, you won't have a chance. The very least they will charge you with, is aiding and abetting the murder of your mother. You need to…'

'I can't,' said McKenzie, turning to West, her shoulders quivering, 'tell him Sergeant, I can't, I didn't…'

'Lorna…'

'No comment. I can't…'

'Lorna…'

'He'll kill me,' said McKenzie, tears streaming down her face, 'he said…'

'Who?' said West. 'Who said he'd kill you?'

McKenzie, lips sealed, sobbed into the blanket. Munro hung his head and gave her a moment to calm down.

'You have a wonderful sense of loyalty, lassie,' he said, his voice barely audible, 'and I admire you for that, but it's now bordering on stupidity. For the avoidance of doubt, we have proof that the hair found on your mother's coat belongs to you. The fingerprints lifted from the envelope we retrieved from your mother's room, belong to you. And we have CCTV footage that shows you at her apartment around the time she died. The evidence is circumstantial, I admit, but it's stacked against you, Lorna. Now, I don't believe you're guilty, I don't think you have it in you, but a decent brief could easily turn a jury against you, and if it that happens, trust me, you'll not be out before your fiftieth.'

The colour drained from McKenzie's face as she gawped, wide-eyed at West, pleading for a way out.

'Are you joking me?' she said, her voice quavering.

'It's not something I'd joke about,' said Munro.

'But he made me promise, he said … he said no-one would find out.'

'Who, Lorna?' said West, her frustration turning to anger. 'Who, Goddammit?'

McKenzie pushed herself against the wall and curled up like a scolded, frightened child as West and Munro waited patiently for her to speak. She wiped her face with the blanket and pulled it tight around her shoulders in the hope it might protect her.

'He … he told me to get rid of Mammy's stuff,' she said, her breath short, gasping as she spurted out the words, 'he said I had to lose the paperwork or…'

Munro, startled, held up his hand and paused the conversation.

'Why?' he said. 'Why would he say that, Lorna? I mean, you were the one stealing the money. Did he put you up to it?'

'No, I was doing it before we met.'

'So, why was he so concerned?'

'I don't know,' said McKenzie, 'I just thought he was being … protective, you know? He said we had all the information we needed, he said we didn't need the statements, or the letters, or the bank cards. He said if anyone ever found out, it would be too incriminating.'

'And you were scared?' said Munro.

'Terrified. I told you, he said … he said if I ever told anyone about the money, he'd do me.'

'Had he threatened you before?' said West.

'No, but he has this knack, this talent, for making you feel…'

'So, what happened next?'

'He told me to meet him, it was late…'

'Where? At Dunmore House?' said Munro.

'No, no, Main Street, by the path that leads through the glen.'

'And?'

'He gave me the keys.'

'Your mother's keys?' said West.

'Aye.'

'And you didn't think to ask where he'd got them?'

'No,' said McKenzie, 'I was petrified, I just … I just took them. He said I was to hide the paperwork in her flat, somewhere not too obvious.'

'Okay,' said Munro, 'so you went to the flat, and that's

when Mrs. Fraser…'

'Aye. She was good. She could've called the police, but she didn't. It was almost like she knew who I was.'

'And did she?'

'No, of course not, I mean, I don't think so.'

Munro took a deep breath and smiled, sympathetically, at McKenzie.

'This fellow,' he said, 'the chap you're in cahoots with, he wouldn't happen to be your boyfriend now, would he? The older boyfriend? The divorced boyfriend?'

McKenzie's cheeks flushed with guilt.

'Lorna,' said West, joining her on the bunk, 'did he ever ask you for any money?'

'No,' said McKenzie, 'apart from a tenner once, so's we could get a few tinnies.'

'And to your knowledge, he's never tried to access your mother's account?'

'No.'

'But he knows how much there is?'

'Aye.'

'And he has all her details?'

'Aye.'

'But you still won't tell us who he is?'

McKenzie shook her head.

Munro sat back, folded his arms and turned his attention the woefully small window set high up, near the ceiling.

'The day before your mother was found,' he said, 'you went to see your daddy, I mean, Callum. Is that right?'

'Aye,' said McKenzie, 'I go most weekends. He likes to cook. If you can call it that.'

'And does he know you're in to DIY?'

'DIY? Me? What makes you think that?'

Munro rubbed his chin and leaned forward again, his eyes, now cold and hard, drilled into hers.

'Because you borrowed a hammer,' he said, 'and you never returned it.'

McKenzie froze.

'Can you leave now, please,' she said, swallowing hard, 'I think I'm going to be sick.'

'Okay,' said Munro as he stood to leave, 'we'll leave you be. And Lorna, I'm going to arrange a lawyer for you, because, trust me lassie, you're going to need one. You're going to need the best we can get.'

* * *

'Talk about stubborn,' said West as they left the cells, 'he must have some hold over her if she's willing to take the blame for him.'

'Right enough,' said Munro, 'probably some low-life who'll not hesitate in breaking her jaw if she so much as utters his name.'

'Maybe she thinks she'll be safer behind bars.'

'It's certainly possible, Charlie, no doubt about that. Perhaps a visit from Mr. Kappelhoff will cheer her up.'

Chapter 18

West was not materialistic, nor was she easily impressed, but, as Munro held the key fob aloft and the lights flashed on the silver BMW 5 Series saloon parked across the street, she couldn't help but smile at the prospect of getting behind the wheel.

'No chance,' said Munro.

'Oh, come on,' said West as they crossed the road, 'I'll look after it, I've never driven anything as stylish as that.'

'Stylish? Och, lassie, it's an ostentatious, over-priced lump of metal, there's nothing stylish about it.'

'Maybe you're right,' said West as she opened the passenger door and clocked the mess in the foot well, 'bloody hell, has this been used on a stake-out in Bethnal Green? It's a bleeding tip.'

'Aye, smells like one, too,' said Munro, turning his nose up the scent of cheap perfume and stale cigarette smoke, 'there's one thing to be said about that Mr. MacDonald, he's a classy date.'

'Never had Nick down as a junk food addict,' said West as she bent down to scoop up the burger wrappers and discarded cups, 'I always thought…'

She stopped, mid-sentence, and stared at one of the

paper cups before turning her attention to the seat and then the headrest.

'What is it, Charlie?' said Munro, sensing her unease.

'Not here,' she said, quietly, as she climbed in the back seat, 'let's go.'

* * *

The car park adjacent to the railway station, though large enough to accommodate the needs of a sprawling conurbation, was rarely busy, frequented, as it was, more by shoppers than commuters. Munro parked alongside a white Transit van, sheltered from the prying eyes of the security cameras, and turned to face West. With her sleeve pulled over her hand to avoid contamination, she held up a paper cup.

'Look at the straw,' she said, 'the lipstick. When I met her, Maureen Connolly was wearing pink lipstick.'

'So,' said Munro, 'women change their lipstick as often as they change their minds, do they not?'

West glowered.

'Women of a certain age do not,' she said, 'they know what works for them.'

'Okay,' said Munro, 'joshing aside, this is bright red. What of it?'

'Oh, come on James, don't tell me you're losing your touch. McKenzie!'

Munro, his forehead as furrowed as an autumn field, hesitated as though waiting for the punchline to a particularly amusing tale, before howling with laughter.

'Are you joking me?' he said. 'Nick? A senior police officer, and Lorna McKenzie? I've not heard anything so ludicrous before in my entire life! It's incredulous, Charlie! Aye, that's the word, incredulous!'

West stared back, unflinchingly.

'Look at the headrest,' she said, 'the hair on the headrest, it's not peroxide blonde is it?'

Munro conceded to himself that it was definitely more red than blonde and fell silent as he contemplated the accusation.

'You're serious, aren't you?' he said.

'Deadly.'

Munro jumped from the car, walked to the rear and popped open the boot. They stood side by side, and scoured the mountain of junk seemingly dumped there at random: a pair of mud-encrusted Wellington boots, a bright yellow police-issue jacket, a roadside hazard warning triangle, a golfing umbrella, foot-pump, first aid kit, one bottle of coolant and one of screen wash, two litres of engine oil and countless, discarded carrier bags. Munro pulled a pair of gloves from his pocket, snapped them on, and lifted the jacket with his forefinger, sighing as it revealed a rucksack. A small, black rucksack.

'I sincerely hope this contains a kagool and a half-empty flask of tea,' he said as he carefully unzipped it.

'Uh-oh,' said West as she spied the carton of cigarettes.

'Duty Free,' said Munro, 'German. Three packs missing, and, oh dear, a set of house keys.'

'This is serious shit, what the hell...?'

Munro raised a hand as the phone warbled in his pocket.

'Duncan,' he said, 'what's occurring?'

'Chief, there's something...'

'Duncan, hold on, just a minute, you sound like you're in a wind tunnel, are you not in the office?'

'No chief,' said Reid, 'I'm outside, getting soaked, I cannae talk in there.'

'What is it?'

'Email, incoming, someone's just transferred 250 grand to a different account.'

Munro's face dropped as he stared blankly at West.

'What? But that doesnae make any sense,' he said, agitated, 'who could...? How could ... does the email have details of the recipient's account?'

'You mean the sort code and stuff? Aye, it's all there,

everything but a name and address.'

'Good. Okay, Duncan, listen carefully,' said Munro, 'you need to make an excuse to go home, understand? Just for an hour, can you do that?'

'Aye chief, nae bother, then what?'

'Contact the Raiffeisen, tell them to freeze the account, then find out who's got the money; easy enough, right?'

'Roger that, chief. I'm on it.'

'I'm right, aren't I? He's in it up to his neck, isn't he?' said West as Munro put his phone away.

'It's looking like that Charlie, but the only evidence we have suggests that he and Lorna may be in some kind of relationship, it doesnae prove he took the money or had anything to do with Freida's death.'

'Well, what are we waiting for? Come on, we need to get back and see Lorna.'

'Och, Charlie, now who's losing it?' said Munro. 'We cannae do that while Nick's in the building. No, we'll have to wait. Look, put that straw and the hair in the paper bag, we need to get it tested, quick. Kappelhoff will have to wait.'

'What about the rucksack, and the fags, and the...?'

'No, no, we cannae remove anything that might arouse suspicion, Charlie, we have to leave it where it is.'

* * *

The stench of disinfectant and the sound of rubber-soled shoes squeaking on the polished linoleum floor was enough to make Munro sneer.

'I hate hospitals,' he said, as they waited in reception, 'you come in the front door, you go out the back, and if you're not in a box when you leave, the only thing you're good for is filling an egg timer.'

'You should get a donor card,' said West, dryly, 'some poor soul will be over the moon to have your sense of humour when you've gone.'

A tall, skinny man, dressed in jeans and a t-shirt with a

mop of glistening, jet black hair, caught her eye, causing her to blush.

'Inspector,' said Doctor Clark, 'Sergeant West. How are you?'

'Fine,' said West, coquettishly, 'you look, different, I mean, without your white coat, and that ... hat thing you all wear...'

'Andy,' said Munro, as her words tailed off, 'thanks for seeing us, you'll have to excuse Charlie here, she's been single for far too long.'

'Is that so?' said Clark. 'Well, I think I might have a cure for that.'

'You'll need an antidote, too.'

'So, what's up? Is this to do with the lassie in the burn?'

'Aye, it is,' said Munro, 'things have become a wee bit ... complicated, and I need a favour, urgently.'

'If I can do it, sure,' said Clark as West held up the brown paper burger bag, 'but I'm afraid I don't eat stuff like that.'

'No,' said West, 'nor do I. Often. It's inside, a few strands of hair and some lipstick on a drinking straw. We need a DNA profile, like yesterday.'

'Okay,' said Clark.

'We need to know if it matches a lassie by the name of Lorna McKenzie,' said Munro. 'She's on the system.'

'I'll sort it now; do you want to wait or will I call you?'

'We'll wait,' said Munro, 'over there, in the café, will it...?'

'Quicker than you think, I'll not keep you long.'

* * *

Munro found a table, took a handkerchief from his pocket and wiped it down as he studied the mob of dour-looking customers, tucking into doughnuts and bacon sandwiches, with a disparaging eye. West, sporting a mischievous grin, arrived with two cappuccinos and sat opposite.

'Charlie,' he said, 'we're surrounded by folk killing themselves with sugar and fat, can you not look suitably morose?'

'Difficult,' she said, sipping her coffee, 'I think I might be...'

'Och, not Doctor Clark, surely?'

'I think he's a bit of a hunk, actually.'

'A hunk?' said Munro. 'The man needs fattening up. You should introduce him to one of your kebabs.'

'I don't think that would go down too well, somehow.'

'Let me get this right, first you go on a date with a chap who finds dead bodies, now you want to go out with someone who cuts them open.'

'Like to get the full picture,' said West, sarcastically, 'both sides of the coin, if you know what I mean.'

'Be sure and tell me if it doesnae work out,' said Munro, reaching for his phone, 'I've a friend who's a funeral director. Duncan, what is it?'

'It's not good, chief,' said Reid, 'we need to talk, urgently, somewhere private, I mean, this is front page news, you'll not believe...'

'Calm yourself, Duncan. Where are you, now?'

'Just left home, on my way back to the office.'

'Right,' said Munro, 'let me think. Charlie, what time is it?'

'Half one, almost.'

'Dammit. Duncan, has Potato Head fixed my car, yet?'

'Aye, chief,' said Reid, 'raring to go, although, when I say raring, I mean, a car like that...'

'I've no time for jokes, Duncan. Drive it here, quick as you can. We're at the hospital.'

* * *

Munro checked his watch for the umpteenth time as he paced impatiently back and forth outside the main entrance, wincing as Reid screeched to a halt beside him.

'Nothing wrong with the brakes, chief,' he yelled, through the open window, 'I never knew a car like this could...'

'Duncan,' said Munro sternly, as he hopped in the passenger seat, 'this vehicle has more in common with a hearse than a Subaru, so I'll thank you to treat it as such. Now, park up over there, if you please.'

Constable Reid, heeding the warning, trundled to a halt beside a silver BMW. Munro threw back his head and sighed.

'Are you okay, chief?' said Reid.

'No, Duncan, I am not, and I don't suppose you're about to make things any better, are you?'

'I doubt it.'

'Why not try?' said Munro. 'Tell me the 250 grand transferred from Freida's account went out as a standing order.'

'No, 'fraid not.' said Reid. 'It was a one-off.'

'Okay, then please tell me the recipient was Miss Lorna McKenzie.'

'Wrong again.'

'Well, that proves it then.'

'Proves what?' said Reid, perplexed.

'Positivity. It's not what it's cracked up to be. It's Nick, isn't it?'

Reid's shoulders slumped as he stared, aghast, at Munro.

'How the hell did you know that?' he said. 'I mean, Jesus, have you got a sixth sense or something? I cannae believe...'

'You know how serious this is, don't you?' said Munro, lowering his voice.

'Aye, of course, it's deadly...'

'Then, you need to stay calm and say nothing. Got that, Duncan? Not a word.'

'You can rely on me, chief.'

'I know I can, laddie. That's why you're here. Okay,

look, take these keys; that BMW there, it belongs to Nick. Drive it back and park it as discreetly as possible, try not to let him see you. We'll be along shortly.'

* * *

Munro, surprised to find his seat occupied by Doctor Clark, squeezed his way past the line of customers queuing for an early grave as West, toying with her empty coffee cup, flirted with him shamelessly.

'Good grief,' he muttered under his breath, 'she'll be wanting a hotel room in a minute.'

'Inspector,' said Clark, commandeering a chair from the next table, 'here, can I get you a coffee?'

'No, thanks Andy,' said Munro, 'you've not done that already, surely? We're still waiting on results from a few days ago.'

'It's all about resources,' said Clark, 'we've got them, and we're not using them. Afraid you'll have to wait a wee bit longer for results on the hair, though, but as for the lipstick, she's your girl.'

'You're sure, now? Lorna McKenzie?'

'One and the same.'

'Okay, listen, thanks. We have to go just now and dinnae worry about the hair, we've got what we need.'

* * *

'So,' said Munro, as they made their way to the car, 'when's your next appointment with Dr. Feelgood, then?'

'I cancelled it,' said West, tickled by the comment.

'Really? I was under the impression you…'

'Oh, I still think he's a bit of a hunk, problem is, he's also a veggie, and a jogger, and he lives alone, with two cats. Not many boxes ticked there, eh?'

'Not to worry, Charlie, there's always the undertaker, I understand embalming can be quite intoxicating.'

West fastened her seatbelt and watched the wipers as they stuttered and juddered across the windscreen, clearing away the last drops of rain.

'So, are you going to tell me,' she said, 'or do I have to

guess?'

'You already know,' said Munro, despondently, 'and Duncan's just confirmed it. I've called Isobel. I'm away to see her right after I've dropped you back.'

'Not nice when it's one of your own, is it?' said West.

'No Charlie, it is not.'

'What do you want me to do now?'

'Speak to Lorna. Maybe this'll convince her to come clean.'

* * *

McKenzie was not the frightened girl West had left curled up on the bunk just a few hours earlier. There was an air of self-assured confidence about her and a look of ruthless determination on her face.

'Lorna,' said West, 'are you okay?'

'Aye, I'm good,' said McKenzie, 'very good. And I've been thinking, I want to…'

'How long have you been seeing Inspector McGreevy?'

McKenzie, staggered by the ferocity of the statement, was rendered speechless.

'I'll ask again. You and Nicholas McGreevy…'

'I heard you,' said McKenzie, 'I … sorry, I'm just, astounded. How on earth…?'

'It's what I do. So. Do you want to talk?'

'Aye. That's what I was about to say, I want to…'

'Off the record, or are you going to make it official?'

'Official. I want to make a statement. A proper statement.'

'Good for you,' said West, with a comforting smile, 'you've made the right choice. We'll go to the interview room. Constable Reid will be joining us. Well done.'

Chapter 19

Crawford, having cleared her diary in anticipation of his arrival, stood idly by the window and watched as Munro's vintage 304 pulled into the car park. She allowed herself the vaguest of smiles as he carefully locked the door, wiped a smudge from the bonnet and headed inside.

'Isobel,' he said, as he breezed in without knocking, 'I hope I've not put you out, I didnae give you much warning…'

'It's fine, James, honestly,' said Crawford, pulling on her coat.

'I'm not keeping you am I? If you have to go, if you've somebody waiting…'

Crawford laughed.

'There's nobody waiting for me, James, nobody and nothing but a DVD, a bottle of Merlot and a thin crust pepperoni. Don't suppose you like pepperoni, do you?'

'I do not.'

'Should've guessed. No, I just thought, if you need to talk, maybe we could go to a…'

'Sorry Isobel, no,' said Munro. 'What I have to say is best said right here, I cannae risk somebody overhearing.'

'Intriguing,' said Crawford, removing her coat, 'oh

well, in that case, come on then, why all the secrecy?'

Munro closed the door, clasped his hands firmly behind his back and strode purposefully towards the window. He turned and took a deep breath.

'I'll try and keep this simple,' he said, 'but you might want to pour yourself a drink.'

'Just a wee bit early for me, James.'

'Please yourself. Freida Kappelhoff, née Brandt, was married to Ruben, the cobbler. They divorced and she shacked up with Callum McKenzie, with whom she had a child, right?'

'Right.'

'Wrong. Freida was already pregnant when she moved in with Callum. Lorna McKenzie is Ruben's daughter, not Callum's.'

'Well, well,' said Crawford. 'Go on.'

'As you know, Lorna's been charged with fraud, theft and deception for pillaging her mother's bank account – her wealthy, and all but estranged, mother's bank account. Now, see here, Lorna's boyfriend discovered what she was up to; whether Lorna told him herself, we've yet to find out, but, he's been, well, "bullying" might be too strong a word, let's say he's been "coercing" her into doing what he says, which includes divulging Freida's account details.'

'I understand what you're saying, James,' said Crawford, 'but I'm at a loss as to the relevance. This is all about the money, aren't you losing sight of the purpose of this investigation? Freida's death?'

'Trust me, Isobel, it's all relevant. Her boyfriend has just transferred 250 grand from Freida's account, to his own.'

'Bloody hell, and you've got evidence of that? Enough to charge him?'

'Oh, aye,' said Munro, 'we've got the evidence, alright, but I also believe he was responsible for Freida's death.'

Crawford sat up and regarded Munro inquisitively.

'Can you prove that, James,' she said, 'I mean, that's a

serious…'

'Not yet, but I will,' said Munro. 'See, I know for a fact that Lorna met her boyfriend by the glen the night Freida was killed. I also know she went to her mother's apartment, at his behest, to hide all the paperwork from the bank, and…'

'And what?'

'I'm all but certain she took the hammer used in the assault on Freida from Callum's house and gave it to him that same night. I'm just hoping she admits as much in her statement. She's with Charlie, now.'

'Okay, well then, I don't see what's stopping you,' said Crawford, 'why not just go ahead and…?'

'Lorna's boyfriend,' said Munro, heaving a sigh, 'is Nick. Nick McGreevy.'

Crawford, dumbfounded by the accusation, gasped as she fell back in her seat and gawped, open mouthed, about the room, struggling to find the words to respond.

'I … I don't know what to say,' she said, devastated. 'Are you sure? Are you absolutely positive it's…?'

'Isobel. I wouldnae be here if I had any doubts.'

'I think I will have that drink after all.'

Crawford dragged herself from her chair, poured a large scotch and knocked it back in one.

'Christ Almighty,' she said, 'Nick? I just … I just can't believe it. Does he … I mean, has he any idea that you're…'

'No,' said Munro, 'he hasn't a clue. To be honest, if wasn't for the fact he'd pressured me into trying to force a confession from Lorna, I might have had second thoughts about…'

'He did what?'

'Aye, it was, to say the least, disappointing. Very disappointing. Bottom line, Isobel, he's been using Lorna all along, and now that he's got what he wants, well…'

'Poor kid, she must be…'

'Worst part is, she thought they had something

special, she hadn't a clue he was already in a relationship with another woman…'

'The little bastard.'

'…a Miss Maureen Connolly. Owns The Oak Bar on the main road.'

Crawford poured herself another drink and sat down.

'So,' she said, still reeling, 'how do you want to play this?'

'I want to bring him in. Now. This evening,' said Munro, 'arrest him on theft and hold him on suspicion of murder.'

'Okay.'

'I need his car impounded too, there's a mountain of evidence in the boot and, I dare say, a wee search of his house wouldnae go amiss, either.'

Crawford threw her head back and closed her eyes.

'Oh, this is painful, James,' she said. 'Alright, fine, do what you have to do, just keep me informed, okay? Every step of the way.'

* * *

West, as restless as a junkie craving an overdue fix, squirmed in her seat, unable to concentrate on anything at all. Campbell, captivated by the amusing spectacle, looked on as she checked her phone, swore and took a brisk walk around the office in the vain hope the words "missed call" would appear on the screen by the time she returned to her desk.

'Are you okay, Charlie?' he said, 'you seem awful tense, edgy even. Can I get you something? Cup of tea, maybe?'

'No thanks, Iain. I'm fine, really. It's just the waiting, it's such a bloody nuisance when…'

The ring tone cut her short.

'James!' she said, with a sigh of relief, 'I've been waiting an age, has Isobel…?'

'It's all go, lassie,' said Munro, 'how about Lorna? Did she…'

'Like a canary, as they say. We've got it all, James, everything: the affair with Nick and his controlling behaviour, how he threatened her and, she's even admitted to taking the hammer from Callum's place…'

'Excellent, but did she say why she took…?'

'Nick of course, it's obvious, he didn't want to use anything that could be traced back to him. She gave it to him, the night they met at the glen.'

'Okay. Now listen Charlie, one more thing. Ask her if she knows of Nick's whereabouts the night before Freida died, it's crucial.'

'No problem, any particular reason…'

'Och, Charlie, come on. He and Freida knew each other, they were pals. They must have met, how else would he have laced her drink? Now, where's Iain? Is he about the place?'

'Yup, he's sitting opposite…'

'Right, the pair of you, meet me at Nick's place in half an hour, got that?'

Chapter 20

The house, an anonymous-looking semi in a quiet cul-de-sac lined with fifteen other identical, characterless properties, was the only one without a manicured front lawn. Instead, in its place, lay a vast expanse of black tarmac upon which sat a five-door, silver BMW. Munro pulled up twenty yards short of the drive and contemplated the imminent confrontation as the streetlights flickered into life and cast a warm, yellow glow across the otherwise bleak, grey street. His voice was soft and low as he answered the call.

'Charlie,' he said, 'is everything alright?'

'Yeah, nothing to worry about,' said West, 'we'll be there in fifteen. Just thought you should know, Lorna says Nick was with her in Paisley the night before Freida copped it, but he didn't get there till late, gone ten.'

'Did he stop?'

'Yup, he was there all night.'

* * *

McGreevy, clutching a can of lager and still in uniform, minus the tie and epaulettes, was clearly not expecting visitors.

'James,' he said, taken aback, 'what brings you here?

Has something…'

'We need a wee chat,' said Munro, bluntly, 'best not do it on the doorstep, eh?'

Declining the offer of a beer and a seat, Munro allowed McGreevy to make himself comfortable in his favourite leather armchair before continuing.

'You've that look about you, James,' he said, 'the one you have just before the proverbial's about to hit the fan.'

'Then think of me as the proverbial, Nick,' said Munro, glibly, 'and you, the fan.'

'You've lost me.'

'Lorna McKenzie.'

'Aye. What of her?'

'How long have you two been seeing each other?'

McGreevy spluttered as he choked on the beer.

'What?' he said, wiping his mouth with the back of his hand.

'You and McKenzie. Och, Nick, there's no point denying it, we…'

'Denying it?' said McGreevy, defiantly, as he shifted uncomfortably in his seat. 'There's nothing to deny. What makes you think…'

'We have her statement,' said Munro.

'She's just a kid, what would I be doing with…'

'She's told us everything.'

'Told you…? I don't believe I'm hearing this,' said McGreevy, 'told you what?'

'Everything. You and her. Your wee … dalliance.'

'Dalliance? God in heaven, are you losing it James? Can you not see she's clearly making it up?' said McGreevy, forcing a nervous laugh.

'And why would she do that?'

'I told you, she's deranged, you should've listened to me and called the shrink when you had the…'

'We've proof, Nick,' said Munro. 'We have her DNA. Taken from your car,'

'You really are pushing it now…'

'And she says you were with her the night before Freida died. In her flat.'

McGreevy stood up, crushed the beer can and held it tight in his fist.

'Utter tosh,' he said, scowling, 'I've not heard anything so preposterous in my entire life, I don't even know where she lives.'

'No? Och, well, that is shame then,' said Munro, 'seems you've just talked yourself out of an alibi. I've an idea, what say we change the subject? Let's talk about the money.'

McGreevy froze.

'What money?' he said, nervously scratching the back of his crew cut head.

'The money, Nick, the money. By Jiminy, I'm losing my patience now, the 250 thousand pounds that miraculously appeared in your bank account.'

'I've not checked my statement,' said McGreevy facetiously, 'I wouldn't know.'

Munro, eyes narrowed, fixed him with an ice-cold stare.

'Okay, Nick, I've done my best,' he said, 'you've had your chance…'

'Chance?' said McGreevy menacingly, through clenched teeth. 'Chance? See here, James, there's only one chancer here, and that's you. Now, take your holier-than-thou attitude and your… your false allegations, and get the hell out of my house. Oh, and I'll tell you this for nothing, pal, come the morning, mark my words, I'll be gunning for you, you'll be out of a job before…'

'I am out of a job, Nick,' said Munro as the doorbell rang, 'you forget, I'm retired. Wait here.'

Munro returned, followed by West and a dour-looking Campbell.

'Oh, not you too, Iain?' said McGreevy, in disbelief. 'Surely not. What's going on here? Is this some kind of conspiracy?'

'There's no conspiracy, sir,' said Campbell, pulling the handcuffs from his belt, 'just evidence, plain and simple.'

Munro stood to one side and cleared his throat.

'Nicholas McGreevy,' he said, 'much as it pains me to do so, I am arresting you for... och, Charlie, you do it, I cannae be bothered, I have a bad taste in my mouth. Iain, cuff him and give him a lift to ours.'

'I'll not need restraining,' said McGreevy, reaching for his coat and another can of beer, 'I still have my dignity.'

'That's about all you have,' said Munro, 'for now at least, anyway.'

* * *

West sat silently on the arm of the sofa as a solemn stillness filled the air, and regarded a disheartened Munro with an empathetic smile.

'That can't have been easy,' she said softly, 'bit like finding out your fiancé's done the dirty on you.'

'Och, I don't think it's as bad as that, Charlie,' said Munro, knowingly, 'it's more like a bereavement, the passing of someone you once knew. Or thought you knew. Still, no point in moping lassie, come on, chop, chop, we've work to do.'

'Okay,' said West, 'what about the car? Shall I call forensics?'

'No, no. I think we'll spare him the embarrassment of having them pull it to pieces in full view of the neighbours,' said Munro, 'you can drive it back, we'll do it at the office.'

'Right, well in that case, we'll have this for starters,' said West, bagging a laptop, 'let's see what else we can find.'

West turned her attention to the sideboard, opened the bottom drawer and rifled through an assortment of DVDs and CDs as Munro cast an eye over the room.

'This is not so much a bachelor pad,' he said, observing the blank, magnolia walls and empty shelves, 'it's more like a cell, in solitary. What've you got there?'

'Nothing yet,' said West, closing the second drawer, 'just a boxed cutlery set and some linen napkins.'

'Dear God, as if he's one for entertaining.'

'Hold on,' said West, 'here we go, utility bills, DVLA, Council Tax demands and, a whole heap of stuff from the bank. Should keep Duncan busy for a while.'

Munro stood beside West as she bagged the contents of the drawer and ran a finger through the dust on the top of the sideboard, eyeing the porcelain bowl filled with loose change, the two biros, one black and one blue, the empty notepad and the portable telephone with integral answering machine. The light flashed on the base station.

'Three messages,' he said. 'Now, why do you suppose he's not listened to them? I mean, he's been home a fair while.'

'Maybe he was here when they called, you know, screening them.'

Munro pressed the button.

"You have three new messages. Message one, sent yesterday at 16,43 hours: Nick, Tommy here, I've some good news, call me back."

Munro looked at West and shrugged his shoulders.

"Message two, sent today at 10,15 hours: Nick, Tommy from McNeill and Partners, call me back, cheers. Message three, sent today at 17,12 hours: Nick, been trying to call you, listen your offer's been accepted on the house in Morningside, well done, I'm sure you and Miss Connolly will be very happy there, give me a call as soon as you get this so's we can get the ball rolling, cheers."

West looked up at Munro and smiled.

'And that,' she said, 'is what we call a motive.'

'Aye, bag that too, would you Charlie? And we best let Miss Connolly know she'll not be moving to Edinburgh any time soon.'

'Right, are we off then?'

'Aye. Now listen, once you've secured the car and called forensics, grab Iain and the two of you take yourselves off to The Oak Bar and invite Miss Connolly over for some tea and cake. I don't care how you do it, illegal use of peroxide, suspicion of short measures, anything, just bring her in, okay? I'll be with Nick.'

Chapter 21

Crawford, still in shock and wishing she'd brought a bottle of scotch to keep her company, sat alone in the side room, diligently watching the small, black and white monitor for any signs of movement. She perked up as Munro, accompanied by Constable Reid, entered from the right of the screen and sat opposite McGreevy.

'For the purpose of the tape,' he said, hitting the voice recorder, 'I am Detective Inspector James Munro, also present in the room are Constable Duncan Reid and the accused, Inspector Nicholas McGreevy.'

Crawford shivered at the unexpected pause as McGreevy and Munro glowered at each other like opponents in a chess match.

'Do you understand why you're here, Nick?' said Munro.

McGreevy, his face as hard as granite, said nothing.

'Do you understand the charges against you?'

McGreevy reached into his breast pocket and, without averting his gaze, produced a business card and pushed it with his index finger across the table.

'My brief,' he said, 'I'll say nothing till he's here.'

Munro, unwilling to entertain a delay of any kind,

continued regardless.

'As you wish,' he said, standing up. 'We'll call him, soon enough. In the meantime, you'll not mind if I think aloud? Ask myself a few rhetorical questions? No? Good. See, I was wondering about the rucksack in the boot of your car. It's a wee, black thing. Did you know Lorna McKenzie has one just like it? Aye, quite a coincidence, wouldn't you say? The unusual thing about it, though, is what was inside. Cigarettes. The kind Freida Kappelhoff brought back from Germany. I never knew you were a smoker, Nick.'

'No comment.'

'I understand your friend, Maureen, enjoys a smoke,' said Munro, as McGreevy flinched. 'Oh, aye, we know about Maureen, Nick. She strikes me as the kind of lady who'll not take kindly to finding out her partner was having a fling with a lassie half her age.'

'No comment,' said McGreevy as his forehead began to glisten with perspiration.

'In fact, I dare say she'll be furious when she discovers she'll not be moving to Edinburgh now; but, the one thing I cannae quite explain, is why, when you already had the money, you had to kill Freida Kappelhoff, I mean, what could you possibly gain by...'

'Now, hold on,' said McGreevy, riled, 'I've killed no-one, if you're insinuating that I...'

'Oh, dear, I appear to have hit a nerve. My, my, Nick, you know I never had you down as murderer, I always thought...'

'Murderer? No, no, no, see, you've got this all wrong, I never...'

'Then why did you meet Lorna that night? By the entrance to the glen?'

'I ... we ...'

'Save your breath, I know why. It's all in Lorna's statement. She brought you the hammer, the one she took from her Daddy's house, just before Freida arrived, then you and she took a lovely wee, moonlit stroll through the glen, and that's when you finished her off…'

'I'll not listen to this! I did not…'

'So there'd be no way anyone could stop you from pilfering her money. Not even Lorna, which is why you were so keen to see her go down for the murder of her mother.'

'That's a blatant lie!' said McGreevy furiously, as he rose to his feet, 'I did not go to the glen, get it? I did not kill Kappelhoff. That wee bitch is setting me up, can you not see that?'

'Then why did you meet her?' yelled Munro.

'To the give her the Goddamn paperwork from the bank! I told her we had to…'

The room fell silent as McGreevy's words tailed off and he slumped back down in his seat.

'Thanks, Nick. That's most … accommodating … of you. I'll phone your lawyer, just now, let him know where you'll be staying.'

'What do you mean?' said McGreevy, fuming at his own stupidity. 'He knows where I…'

'Och, you'll not be stopping here,' said Munro, 'with Miss McKenzie just along the corridor? No, no, I've arranged a nice room for you in Greenock. HMP Greenock. Rooms are a wee bit small but I understand the food is quite acceptable. We'll be along to see you tomorrow.'

* * *

Crawford, looking drained, stood by the open doorway and waited for Munro.

'That was sly,' she said.

'Needs must, Isobel. At least we have him now.'

'He's got quite a temper on him, hasn't he?'

'Aye,' said Munro, 'so would I, if someone had just accused me of murder.'

'What are you saying?' said Crawford, addled by the ambiguity of his answer, 'I thought…'

164

'Theft by deception,' said Munro. 'He's guilty of that, no doubt about it, but murder? I'm not so sure.'

'But all the evidence … I mean, even you said, it all points to…'

'Aye, it does, Isobel, it does, but where's the proof? No, something's not right here.'

'Well, take a break, clear your head,' said Crawford, 'come on, let me buy you a drink, I could murder a bloody large…'

'No, no. Sorry. I've someone to see just now. I'll telephone you later.'

* * *

West, as jaded and as listless as a librarian at a book fair, smiled with relief as Munro finally appeared and joined them at the desk.

'Miss Connolly,' he said with a weary smile, 'I hope I've not kept you long, it's been quite a day so far. Quite a day, indeed.'

'What do you want?' said Connolly, venomously, 'I'm not happy about this, you cannae keep me here, you know? I know my rights.'

'Aye, I'm sure you do,' said Munro, 'and you're right, of course, we cannae keep you here. We're not charging you with anything, and you've not been arrested, so, you're free to go, whenever you like.'

'What?'

'You're free to go. Whenever you like.'

'Right. Good,' said Connolly. 'Maybe I'll just finish my tea first.'

'Okay, and while you do that, you'll not mind if ask a question or two. About Nick.'

Connolly glanced at West and back again.

'Sergeant, here, says he's in a wee spot of bother.'

'Aye, unfortunately, that is the case,' said Munro, with a sympathetic nod. 'Can you tell me about the house?'

'The house? My house?'

'No, no. The one in Morningside.'

'Oh, it's beautiful,' said Connolly, 'big as you like. Has something happened to it?'

'No, but if you don't mind me asking, I need to know how you and Nick were paying for it. Did you have a mortgage?'

'That's none of your business,' said Connolly, slamming down her mug. 'It's a private matter. Between Nick and myself.'

Munro sighed, stood up and slowly walked to the filing cabinet where he pulled a manila folder from the top drawer.

'See this,' he said, waving it casually, 'this…'

'Okay, okay,' said Connolly uneasily, 'I'm selling the bar. I've an offer on the table, and Nick's putting up the rest.'

'He's selling his house?' said West.

'No, he's keeping that. For work, he says. No, he's an aunty on his mother's side, not long passed on. She's left him, well, a tidy sum; put it that way.'

'Is that so?'

'Aye, that's how come we can pay cash.'

'Okay Miss Connolly, look, thanks for coming by,' said Munro, 'I appreciate it, but, a word of advice, if you've not sold the bar yet, I'd take it off the market if I were you.'

'What? Why?'

'Sergeant West will fill you in. After that, you're free to go.'

* * *

The office, save for the light filtering through the blinds from the street lamps outside, was in total darkness. Munro, his face cast in shadow, sat with his elbows on the table, his chin resting on his hands, staring blankly in to space.

'Suits you,' said West.

'What does?'

'The desk. You look quite…'

'Oh, aye? Do I look a pen-pusher, Charlie?'

'Well, you know your way around a filing cabinet,' said West as Munro, frowning, turned to face her. 'What was it? That folder you pulled? The one you were waving to scare the crap out of her?'

Munro smiled.

'I've no idea,' he said, 'I just took the first one I could lay my hands on.'

'You crafty sod! You're one of a kind, you know that?'

'I'll take that as a compliment,' said Munro. 'How was she? Miss Connolly?'

'Furious, to say the least. Wouldn't like to be in his shoes, put it that way. So, come on, you haven't said, how'd it go? With Nick? Have we got him?'

Munro glanced at West, took a deep breath and heaved a sigh.

'He didn't do it, did he?' said West. 'Oh, my God, you don't think it was him?'

Munro simply shook his head.

'Shit. But who else is there? There's no-one else in the frame, it has to be…'

'Sit down,' said Munro, 'I've been thinking,'

West pulled up a chair and sat by the side of the desk.

'Okay, we know Lorna took the hammer, right? And we know she and Nick met by the path to the glen, he's admitted as much himself, but see, here, Nick's not a Neanderthal, he wouldnae bash someone on the head with a hammer, he's too clever for that. I think he went home after he'd handed her the stuff from the bank. I dinnae think it was Nick who went a walk with Freida. I think…'

'Lorna?' exclaimed West. 'You think it was Lorna? Oh, no, come on, her own mother? It's a bit extreme, isn't it? All that just for a few quid?'

'We need to check, Charlie, because unless you've a better idea, I cannae think of anyone else who might have done it. Go fetch her coat and the FLS.'

Munro cleared the desk, pulled the blinds and

snapped on a pair of gloves.

'So,' said West, as she laid out the anorak, 'what are we looking for, exactly?'

'I'm not entirely sure, but if I'm right, something that belongs to Freida.'

Munro slowly guided the FLS over the hood and around the collar.

'Why do I get the feeling we should've done this ages ago?' said West.

'We're not infallible, Charlie, besides, we had no reason to. Och, there's nothing. Turn it round, let's check the sleeves, right arm, around the cuff.'

'There!' said West, excitedly, 'go back. It's not much, but…'

'Could be spatter,' said Munro.

'If it is, will we have enough? Evidence, I mean, to get a conviction?'

'Oh, aye. We've enough, alright. Wounding with intent, at the very least.'

West switched on the lights and leaned against the wall.

'So, if that does turn out to be Freida's blood,' she said, 'I mean, well, it proves Nick's in the clear, doesn't it?'

'Only as far as the assault's concerned. He'll still do time for theft.'

'But what about the poisoning?'

'Aye. The poisoning,' said Munro, as he stuffed the coat into a large, paper bag, 'now that's more his style.'

'Are you saying…?' said West.

'Aye, Charlie, that's exactly what I'm saying. He's our man.'

'Okay, let's run through this,' said West, probingly. 'Why? Why would he poison Freida?'

'To shut her up. Cover his tracks. Look, if she discovered 250 grand had gone missing from her account and reported it to the bank, they'd say where it went.'

'Alright then. But how? When?'

'Well,' said Munro as he perched on the edge of the desk and folded his arms, 'we know he didn't meet Lorna till after ten the night before Freida died.'

'Yes, but do we?' said West. 'I mean, if she's lied about giving Nick the hammer, then she could be lying about that, too.'

'No, no,' said Munro, 'she's no reason to cover for him, quite the opposite, in fact, and according to the Duty Roster, Nick left here around six, so that would've given him a window of four hours, or thereabouts.'

'Yes,' said West, 'but where the hell would he have met her? You can't exactly pour someone a glass of anti-freeze while you're sitting in the pub, and Freida didn't go out that night, she was with Mrs. Fraser, remember? They had their little, soirée, she wouldn't have had time to meet him…'

'Unless,' said Munro, 'he went to her.'

'Come again?'

'Nick. He could easily have gone to Dunmore and hung around for an hour or two before Fraser showed up, and still had time to get to Paisley by ten.'

'Yeah, suppose so,' said West, yawning, 'sorry, my brain's fried, 'so what do we…'

'I need you to do one more thing before you fall asleep and miss out on the largest vodka and tonic you've ever seen.'

'I'm awake, go on, you've got me.'

'Go bat your eyelashes at Doctor Feelgood,' said Munro, thrusting the paper bag into her arms, 'we need a match on this tonight. No need to wait, he can call you when he's got the result. Iain can run you over.'

'Okay, and in the meantime, you are…?'

'Away to see to Mrs. Fraser. I'll meet you at the hotel. In the bar.'

* * *

Munro zipped his jacket against the chill, evening breeze; crunched his way up the gravel drive; checked his watch and, though slightly embarrassed at the late hour, rang the bell and waited. The door was promptly answered by a prim Mrs. Fraser, beaming as though she'd been expecting him.

'Inspector,' she said, standing aside, 'how nice to see you, come in, come in, there's a snell wind about tonight.'

Munro stepped inside, struck at once by the stifling heat.

'Very kind, Mrs. Fraser,' he said. 'Look, apologies for calling so late, I hope I'm not disturbing your supper or...'

'No, no, I'm just up to a wee bit of tidying, that's all. Can I get you a...?'

'No, thanks,' said Munro, 'I'll not keep you long. I just need to ask you a couple of very brief questions, if that's alright?'

'Of course,' said Fraser, 'fire away.'

'Last week, the night before Freida ... the night you and Freida had your wee ... get together...'

'Yes?'

'I realise this may sound odd, but I don't suppose you know if Mr. McGreevy dropped by? Inspector McGreevy?'

'Och, you mean Nick? Why, yes, he did. You look surprised, you needn't be, they go back years, we all do, you know that.'

'Aye, right enough, must've slipped my ... did he stop? Was he here long?'

'About an hour, I'd say,' said Fraser, 'he took his leave when I arrived.'

'Is that so?'

'Aye, I think he wanted to linger but I must've scared him off.'

'What makes you say that?'

'Well, he'd brought some wine for Freida and it wasn't her birthday, so...'

'I see,' said Munro, 'and did you not think it unusual, him just popping round like that?'

'No, no, Inspector, he and Donald, you know, young

Duncan's father, they do it all the time, I think they both still held a torch for her, even after all these years.'

'Okay, well in that case, I've just one last question then, the wine. Would you happen to … och, no, it's too much to ask.'

'Try me, Inspector, I'm not bad in the head, not yet.'

Munro laughed gently.

'Okay,' he said, 'the wine,'

'Riesling.'

'Screw top or cork?'

'Screw.'

'Open, or…'

'Open.'

'And…'

'A little acidic, I thought.'

'You drank it?' said Munro, surprised.

'Oh, aye,' said Mrs. Fraser, 'well, just a wee sip, actually. It wasn't what I'd call, palatable, and I'm not keen on white anyway, I prefer my Tempranillo. Freida didn't seem to mind though.'

'She drank it? All?'

'Pretty much, then the Pinot.'

'Pinot?'

'Yes, I brought a bottle of red for me, and the Pinot for Freida.'

'I see, okay, and what about the bins?' said Munro. 'I imagine they'd have been emptied by now?'

'Och, if it's the bottles you're after, Inspector, we didn't have a chance to throw them out, those friends of yours, the forensic chappies, they took them away.'

* * *

The bar, though annoyingly busy, proved a welcome distraction for Munro, offering, as it did, an opportunity to forget about work. Instead, he chose to castigate the owner for the deafening music, the clientele for their raucous behaviour, and the restaurant for threatening to stop serving food because this kitchen was about to close, a problem he resolved with a wave of his badge. His lip curled in disgust as the barman set down a large scotch and a vodka and tonic, and slid a half empty bowl of dry-roasted peanuts towards him. West, like a terrier on a scent, snaked her way through the crowd and claimed her prize.

'That,' she said with a satisfied gasp, 'is going down far too easily.'

Munro gestured to the barman for another.

'So,' he said, as West grabbed a fistful of nuts, 'och, lassie, not those, please.'

'Why, what's up?'

'What's up? The whole bar's had their fingers in that bowl.'

'So?'

'And where do you suppose those fingers were, before they went in there?'

'Oh, gross,' she said, tipping them back. 'Good point.'

Munro sipped his scotch.

'So,' he said, 'how was Dr. Feelgood? Hope he didnae affect your blood pressure.'

'No chance of that,' said West, 'he was quite peeved actually, didn't take kindly to me interrupting his chat-up lines with a tiny, blonde bit on reception. He'll call. How about you?'

'Better than I thought. Seems our Nick did go to see Freida, after all.'

'You're kidding?' said West, impressed. 'Bloody hell Sherlock, how do you do it?'

'He was there for an hour, took some wine, German incidentally, and Freida pretty much had it all to herself.'

'So, did you grab the bottle? Don't tell me they threw…'

'I did not,' said Munro, 'but forensics did. That's what we're waiting on.'

'Still? Why the delay?'

'Who knows, lassie? Perhaps they're French. Now, I

cannae abide this racket any longer and I assume you're hungry?'

'What do you think? I'm bloody famished.'

'Good, I've got a table in the restaurant and a couple of sirloins on the go.'

'James Munro, if you were twenty years younger...'

Chapter 22

West, feeling fresh after a solid night's sleep, woke early, stretched and smiled to herself as she gazed out across the Clyde from the bedroom window. The sun was breaking over the horizon, illuminating the soft, fluffy underbelly of the scattered, white clouds, causing her to contemplate, in the absence of any plans for the future, postponing her return to London. She checked her phone. One missed call. Andy Clark. One text message, succinct and to the point: "Jacket. Match positive. Freida Kappelhoff".

* * *

Munro was alone in the restaurant, cradling a cup of tea while he waited for his breakfast to be served, when an excitable West rushed in and plonked herself down opposite him.

'Guess what?' she said, grinning.

Munro, nonplussed, answered matter of factly.

'McKenzie's coat,' he said. 'Spatter matches Freida's DNA.'

'How the hell did you know?' she said, deflated.

'I got a wee text from Andy too.'

'So, when do we tell her? Charge her? Lorna?'

'Just as soon as we've had our breakfast.'

* * *

Constable Reid, armed with a roll of kitchen towel and a bottle of anti-bacterial spray was, in an effort to stave off an impending bout of boredom, busying himself by polishing the front desk and anything else he could lay his hands on. He stopped, grateful for the company, as Munro, whistling the theme to The Great Escape, skipped through the door with West in tow.

'Och, it's a beautiful morning out there Duncan,' he said, 'simply beautiful.'

'Take your word it for it, chief,' said Reid, 'I'll not get to see it, not unless a major incident involving incendiary devices, several vehicles and a flood of biblical proportions requires my somewhat limited expertise.'

'What nonsense laddie, you've a vast range of skills, all vital to the running of this station,'

'Thanks, chief, I...'

'...and knowing how to make a decent brew is one of them. Has anything happened?'

'No,' said Reid, filling the kettle, 'we're still waiting to hear about a replacement for Inspector McGreevy; it'll be some trumped-up, jobsworth from the city, no doubt.'

'Aye, no doubt,' said Munro, 'Charlie, have a wee word with Duncan, here, would you? Tell him about the power of positivity. Anything else?'

'No,' said Reid, 'I mean yes, Christ, I nearly forgot. Finally got a call back from Kappelhoff's solicitors. Fella by the name of Paterson, says he'd like a wee word.'

'Did he say what about?'

'No, just said it might be relevant, wasnae bothered whether you called him back or not, but he says he's free all morning.'

'Are they nearby?'

'Nearby? Couldn't be closer, chief. McCleary's. Bath Street. Above the bank.'

* * *

Munro, with the sun on his face and his hands behind

175

his back, dawdled up the street as if enjoying a casual stroll in the park.

'What about Lorna?' said West, ambling alongside. 'Shouldn't we be...'

'She's not going anywhere, Charlie. Let's see what this legal eagle has to say for himself first, and let's hope he's not charging us for his time.'

Four minutes later they arrived outside the bank. An old, brass plaque mounted on the wall by the side door, proclaimed 'McCleary & Partners, Solicitors and Commissioner for Oaths'. West glanced through the open door and up the gloomy, unlit stairwell.

'Looks a bit spooky,' she said, 'like the entrance to a haunted house.'

'They do it on purpose,' said Munro, 'a wee reminder that you're about to pass through a portal to hell and surrender all that you hold dear.'

A balding, middle-aged man, with drooping jowls and a belly like Buddha, sat wedged between his desk and the wall, almost hidden by the piles of folders and books stacked precariously about him. Breathing heavily, he struggled to stand as Munro entered the room, gave up and sat down again.

'Can I help?' he said, panting, as he regarded him over the top of his half-moon glasses.

'Mr. Paterson? Detective Inspector Munro, and this is Detective Sergeant West. You telephoned earlier. Freida Kappelhoff?'

'Oh, aye, that's right. Sorry to hear of her passing, tragic circumstances. She was a lovely lady, very polite.'

'You knew her?' said West.

'No, not really,' said Paterson, 'I handled her divorce years back, but that's pretty much it.'

'I see,' said Munro, 'so, what was it, exactly, you wanted to talk about?'

'We had a meeting last week, the Tuesday, it was. No, no, the Wednesday.'

'And?'

'Well, it was all a wee bit, peculiar.'

'What was?' said Munro.

'Everything, really,' said Paterson as he removed his glasses and rubbed his eyes. 'We had an appointment, you see, three o'clock. She said she wanted to make a change to her will. Well, I popped out for my lunch and came back in plenty of time, about 2.30, and there was a wee lassie hanging about on the street outside. I thought nothing of it, but when Miss Kappelhoff arrived, this lassie's followed her into my office and, dear God, quite a hullabaloo, it was. The girl's shouting and screaming like you wouldn't believe.'

'And do you know who she was?' said West.

'Aye, her daughter. Apparently. It was obvious she knew Miss Kappelhoff was here to change her will, and I'll tell you this for nothing, she wasnae happy about it.'

'So, what happened next?' said West.

'I had to eject her from the premises,' said Paterson, shaking his head, 'she was that angry, I told her if she didnae leave, I'd have to call the police.'

'And did she?'

'Aye, in a manner of speaking. Nearly took the door off its hinges.'

'And how was Miss Kappelhoff?' said West. 'Was she, upset?'

'A wee bit shaken, I think. She went after her, came back about twenty minutes later, after that, she seemed fine.'

Munro glanced around the cluttered office, the framed certificates hanging on the wall, the rickety bookcase stuffed to overflowing, and the large, cast-iron safe standing in the corner, serving as a side table.

'Do you happen to know what changes she made to the Will, Mr. Paterson?' he said.

'No, no. That's none of my business. I simply witnessed it, she sealed it and then, I locked it away, but...'

'Go on.'

'Well, it's all supposition, I know, but judging by the way her daughter was acting, I'd say if anyone was going to lose out, it was her.'

'Tell me,' said Munro, 'did Freida appoint you Executor, by any chance?'

'No, that would be her sister, let me think now, Magda?'

'Mathild?' said West, 'Mathild Brandt?'

'Aye, that's her.'

'So, you cannae tell us what's in the Will? You cannae open it?'

'No, no,' said Paterson, 'that would be highly irregular, unethical, immoral, even, but … not illegal.'

'So…?'

'So, I'd feel more comfortable about it if we had her sister's permission, or that of someone in authority.'

'Like…'

'Like the Procurator Fiscal, perhaps.'

'I admire your professionalism, Mr. Paterson,' said Munro, 'perhaps it would be best all round, then, if Mathild Brandt gave us her blessing. Are you in contact with her?'

'Oh, aye.'

'Then, would you mind…'

'Nae bother. I'll call her just now; let you know what she says.'

'Okay, just one more thing – out of curiosity, more than anything else,' said Munro, 'did Freida not use her maiden after the divorce? I mean…'

'No, she made that clear in the decree, she wanted to be known as Kappelhoff.'

'Was there any particular reason?'

'I've no idea. Sentiment, that's usually the case.'

* * *

West shielded her eyes from the blinding sun as they emerged from the gloom of the building and headed back

178

to the station.

'Are you thinking what I'm thinking?' she said.

'That he needs a bigger chair?' said Munro.

'Apart from that,' said West. 'That Lorna thought she was going to lose her inheritance, so she and Nick colluded to bump her off before she could change the Will…'

'Aye, and when Freida was still on her feet despite consuming a bottle of anti-freeze…'

'Lorna took matters in to her own hands and decided to finish her off.'

'Sadly, she was already too late. What a waste, Charlie. What a terrible waste.'

* * *

McKenzie, now comfortable in the presence of her captors, sat, quite relaxed, unperturbed by the austere surroundings of the interview room.

'Can I have my coat back, soon?' she said gleefully. 'Gets a wee bit chilly down there.'

'We'll get you another,' said West, with a smile.

'Another? No, I'd rather mine, if it's all the same.'

'I'm afraid not,' said Munro, 'you see, Lorna, your coat is now being held as evidence.'

'Evidence? I don't follow.'

'You've not been entirely straight with us, have you, Lorna?' said West.

'I'm sorry?'

'Your coat. We've had it analysed and we found traces of something on the sleeve. Traces of something that shouldn't be there.'

'Like what?' said McKenzie, laughing. 'Chilli sauce?'

'Close,' said West, 'we found traces of blood. Human blood. Your mother's blood. You didn't pass Nick the hammer when you met by the glen, did you?'

McKenzie bit her lip and glanced nervously around the room.

'You kept it with you. It was you who led your mother

through the glen, and it was you who attacked her, wasn't it?'

McKenzie nodded as a stream of tears flowed down her cheeks and fell silently to her lap.

'So, why did you do it?' said Munro. 'Was it about her Will?'

'You know about that?' said McKenzie, perking up.

'Aye, Lorna, we do. How did you find out your mother planned to change it?'

'She told me. She telephoned me last week. Said I ought to know so's there'd be no surprises when she's gone.'

'And you thought nothing of it?' said West. 'Her changing the Will like that? Out of the blue?'

'Aye, at first I thought she was keeping something from me, like she had the cancer or something, then she said I wasnae fit to have her money, that I didn't deserve it. She went on and on about how she'd tried to make amends, build bridges and that, and all I did was throw it back in her face. Made me feel great, so it did.'

'You were angry, understandably?'

'What do you think? When she told me she was giving it to somebody else, someone who deserved it, I was fair fuming, I mean, how dare she? How dare she give it to someone else over her own flesh and blood?'

'Have you any idea who she was leaving it to?'

'No. Probably some dumb animal charity, knowing her.'

'Well, I'm sure you'll get something, Lorna,' said Munro, 'only problem is, there's not much to spend it on in prison, is there?'

McKenzie stared blankly towards the window, dejected.

'You know where this is going, don't you Lorna?' said West.

'If you're going to charge me,' said McKenzie, 'just get on with it. I dinnae care anymore.'

Chapter 23

Although not averse to the odd surprise, a chance meeting, or encountering the unexpected, Crawford was happier with a degree of regimen in her life, preferring to run to a schedule, thereby knowing exactly what she would be doing, where, when and with whom, at least one week in advance. Interruptions, particularly those occurring within the forty-five minutes that constituted her lunch break, were not well received, unless they involved a delivery from the wine merchant or, as was customary on her birthday, the florist. Munro, however, proved himself to be the exception to the rule. He knocked once and entered without waiting for a reply.

'James!' said Crawford, pleasantly surprised. 'Do we have an appointment? I don't…'

'No, no, Isobel,' said Munro, 'I thought I'd chance it, if you're busy, we could always come back, but…'

'Of course not, come in, sit down. Sergeant West, pull up a chair. So, what's up?'

'A wee update for you. Lorna McKenzie. She's admitted the assault on her mother and she's been charged – wounding with intent.'

'McKenzie?' said Isobel. 'That's a turn up for the

books, I thought you had Nick in the frame for the attack?'

'We did,' said Munro, 'but, it appears Freida changed her Will shortly before she died and Lorna, rightly or wrongly, thought she stood to lose her inheritance…'

'And does she?'

'Aye, reckon so, we'll know for sure, soon enough. The assault was her rather … amateurish … attempt at preventing her mother from changing it, but she was too late.'

'Okay,' said Crawford, 'so, why not attempted murder then?'

'Because, I don't believe she meant to kill her,' said Munro. 'To be honest, the lassie was confused and angry.'

'The prosecution may not see it like that.'

'Aye, right enough, they'll go for the jugular, no doubt about that. In her defence, if Nick knew about the Will, then there may have been a degree of coercion on his part.'

'You think he forced her into doing it?' said Crawford.

'Possibly.'

'And the poisoning? You still think Nick was behind it?'

'Oh, aye,' said Munro. 'We know he visited Freida the night before she died, and he took her a bottle of wine, which she drank by herself. That's how he administered the poison.'

'Good,' said Crawford, 'I assume then, you're going to pay him a visit?'

'Not yet,' said West, 'we're waiting for the test results on the empty wine bottle. If, as we suspect, it proves positive for contamination, then we'll have enough to charge him.'

'And, of course, there's Mrs. Fraser,' said Munro, 'once we have her testimony…'

'Do you think she'll mind?' said Crawford. 'Testifying, I mean? After all, she and Nick, they go back years.'

'Mrs. Fraser's the kind of lady who'd rather do right by Freida than cover Nick's arse. Trust me, she'll be fine.'

'In that case, I won't keep you, and I shan't waste my breath inviting you to lunch either,' said Crawford, smirking as she stood, 'you're probably up to your eyes in it.'

'No, no, there's not too much we can do until the lab…'

Munro winced as West delivered a short, sharp kick to his left ankle.

'What I mean is, you're right, we need to get back, just as soon as we can.'

* * *

Munro, shaking his head, marched swiftly towards the car, handed West the keys and hopped in the passenger seat.

'What was I thinking, Charlie?' he said. 'I must've lost my concentration, she caught me off-guard, she very nearly had me. I'm indebted to you, really, I am. Thanks very much.'

'I never realised she was so desperate.'

'Thanks very much.'

'She really does want to sink her teeth into you, doesn't she?'

'It's not her teeth I'm worried about,' said Munro, 'I mean, I cannae see the attraction, myself, a crinkly, old relic like me doesnae…'

'Oh, come on, you're not that old,' said West, 'besides, it's not all about looks, you know? You're very … enigmatic.'

'Och, not you too, lassie?' said Munro, as he fumbled frantically for his phone, thankful for the timely interruption. West cast him a sideways glance, smiled as he mumbled into the handset, and sighed contentedly as she took in the serenity of the empty, tree-lined carriageway, a million miles from the odorous, over-crowded, noisy streets of Bishopsgate.

'That was Paterson,' said Munro, hanging up, 'Mathild's not due for a couple of weeks yet, but she says it's okay to take a peek at the Will.'

'Excellent,' said West, her mind elsewhere.

'Well, what are you waiting for? This vehicle can travel faster than 30mph, you know?'

'Yeah, I know, but there's no rush, is there?'

Munro huffed, confounded by her sudden lack of urgency and stared through the windscreen as the trees flashed by under a clear, blue sky.

'No, I don't suppose there is, Charlie,' he said, 'I don't suppose there is.'

* * *

Paterson, still stuck behind his desk with a handkerchief tucked into his collar and a trail of curry sauce running down his chin, made no attempt to stand as he hastily pushed a carton of rice to one side and wiped his mouth.

'Sorry,' he said, belching under his breath, 'just having a wee bite to…'

'If we're interrupting…' said West.

'No, you're alright. Anything that stops me eating is welcome here.'

'Well, if you're sure,' said Munro.

'Aye, of course.'

'Have you opened it yet?'

'No, no. Thought you'd like to be present for the unveiling, so I've waited.'

'Okay, well, on you go then,' said Munro, 'let's have a look.'

Paterson pointed to the safe as he downed a pint of water.

'Miss,' he said, 'if you wouldn't mind. Top shelf, tray full of envelopes.'

'Okay,' said West, bending down, 'what's the combination?'

'I've no idea,' said Paterson, 'it's never locked. Just

give the door a wee tug, it's heavier than myself.'

West retrieved a vellum envelope bearing the name 'Freida Kappelhoff', elegantly scripted in indigo ink and underscored with a flourish, and passed it to Paterson.

'Here you go,' she said, 'only right that you should do the honours.'

'Okay,' said Paterson, clearing his throat as he slit the envelope with a stainless steel letter opener, 'and the winner is … och, would you look at that. It's that nice Mrs. Fraser.'

'Mrs. Fraser?' said Munro, frowning as he took the Will. 'The same Mrs. Fraser up at Dunmore?'

'Aye, that's her.'

'She's to get the bulk of the inheritance, with just fifty thousand going to Lorna. Does that not strike you as a wee bit, odd, Mr. Paterson?'

'It's none of my business, Inspector. She must've had her reasons, all I know is, to coin the phrase, she was sound of mind and body when she made the change.'

'Is Mrs. Fraser aware of this?' said West. 'That she's almost a millionaire?'

'I've really no idea,' said Paterson, 'you're forgetting, miss, this is the first time I've seen this, too.'

* * *

Campbell, a beer lover who always regarded his glass as half empty, sat, head on hand, morosely stirring a mug of tea whilst an unusually apathetic Reid, sitting opposite, flicked rolled up pieces of paper across the desk towards a makeshift goal.

'Good grief,' said Munro as they returned to the office, 'what's up with you two? Did Celtic lose again?'

'No,' said Campbell, without looking up, 'we've just had some devastating news, that's all.'

'Oh, dear,' said West, 'I hope it's not, I mean, did somebody die?'

'No, worse than that. The new Inspector's arriving the day after tomorrow, temporary placement till they find someone permanent.'

'Well, that's good, isn't it?'

'No, it's terrible,' said Campbell. 'He's a fella by the name of Hourigan, based in Motherwell.'

'Hourigan?' said Munro. 'No, doesnae ring a bell.'

'It does with me, only it's not so much a bell, more an alarm.'

'Why so?'

'He's not what you might call, a people person. Does things by the book, everything in triplicate, no leeway. Thinks he's in the army.'

'Och, well, a wee bit of discipline Iain,' said Munro, 'there's nothing wrong with…'

'Discipline?' said Campbell. 'He's not a disciplinarian, chief, the man's a control freak. If you dinnae do things his way, then it's the wrong way, and woe betide anyone who begs to differ.'

'I see,' said Munro, 'well, good luck with that, then. We'd like to help, of course, but if all goes to plan, we'll be out of your hair this time tomorrow.'

'I'll be sorry to see you go, chief,' said Reid, 'and you, miss.'

'Ah, thanks Duncan, that's sweet.'

'Chief, I've been thinking, I'm going to sit my exams. There's something about Detective Constable that sounds more exciting than plain, old…'

'Good for you, laddie,' said Munro, grinning, 'you'll make a fine detective, of that I'm sure, now, tell me Duncan, have forensics finished with Nick's car?'

'Aye, all done, it's parked round the back.'

'Good, there's a black rucksack in the boot, inside a set of keys, we need to be sure they belong to Freida, grab them and scoot up to Dunmore would you, and then bag the rucksack as evidence. Charlie, Nick's laptop, let's have a wee look at what he's been up to.'

West opened the MacBook, gave it a second to wake from sleep mode, and looked distinctly surprised at the lack of folders on the desktop.

'It's like it just came out of the box,' she said, 'most people have of tons of folders floating around, you know, photos, work, letters, there's nothing here except the hard drive.'

'Check the browser,' said Iain, 'maybe he just used it for the internet and email.'

West launched Safari and smiled as McGreevy's browsing history for the last seven days cascaded down the screen.

'iPlayer,' she said, 'something I'm not even going to look at, and our favourite bank, here we go.'

'What's up?' said Munro as West, groaning, fell back in her seat.

'Password,' she said, 'we need to log-in. Bugger, we could be here for months.'

'Aye, you're right there,' said Campbell, 'could be anything from his birthday to something to do with McKenzie or Connolly, or, or even a pet, if he had one, and if you cock it up, it may even lock you out altogether.'

Munro wandered slowly but purposefully around the desks, hands clasped beneath his chin as though praying for divine intervention.

'He'd not use anything obvious,' he said, 'not Nick. It'll be something obtuse. Think about it, he's hijacked somebody else's account and he's liberating their life-long savings. Money that would have seen them through their twilight years. It'll be something to do with the future. His future. What has he to look forward to?'

'Not much, now,' said West, 'but, the house, I suppose, in Morningside.'

'Aye, possibly. What else? His retirement, perhaps, but what was he planning...'

Munro stopped, mid-flow, disconcerted by the grin plastered across Campbell's face.

'Is there something amusing about this, Iain? Something I'm not quite getting?'

'No,' said Campbell, 'it's just the thought of the Inspector retiring.'

'What of it?'

'He always referred to it as Linwood. He never said "when I retire", he always said "when I move to Linwood".'

'What's Linwood?' said West. 'Is that a village, or a place, or something?'

'I've no idea,' said Campbell, 'I always thought it was like Dunroamin or something, a name you put outside your…'

Munro held up his hand, cutting him short.

'Linwood,' he said, quietly, 'just outside Glasgow. Armed robbery. Three officers shot, two died. They got away with £14,000.'

'Fourteen grand? That's not much…'

'It was a good few years ago, Iain. Charlie, try "Linwood".'

West carefully keyed in the characters and hit 'return'.

'Oh, well, it was worth a try,' she said, 'although, it does seem a bit short.'

'Short?' said Munro, 'I don't follow.'

'The amount of characters, and they're all letters. Normally, they insist you have a mix of numbers and letters, that sort of thing.'

'Okay, well, try "Linwood1969", that's when it happened, see if that…'

'Genius!' said West, gleefully. 'We're in, now, here we go, look, here's the transfer he made, and if we look here, oh, the greedy bastard, he's scheduled three further payments for the 10th each month, 100k each.'

'Anything on there pertaining to his own account, Charlie? With the Bank of Scotland?'

'Hold on, yup, but we need a password again.'

'Try the same one,' said Munro.

'The same one?'

'Why not? We've nothing to lose.'

'Well, well, well,' said West, 'bit slack for a copper, I bet his pin number's 1969 too. Look at this, the 250 grand transferred from Freida's account, it was withdrawn the following day. Cash.'

'Cash? Where?'

'Blackhall Street. Greenock.'

'Come on,' said Munro, 'get your coat.'

'Where're we going?'

'Nick's place. I doubt he's a wallet large enough for that amount of cash, so it stands to reason he must have it stashed in his house somewhere.'

* * *

Whoever owned the ageing hatchback parked on McGreevy's drive, with its scratched paintwork, broken taillight and missing hub caps, was, thought West, almost certainly missing a valid MOT certificate as well, not to mention a road fund licence and appropriate insurance.

'Shall I call it in?' she said, as Munro cruised past and parked opposite. 'Get Iain to run a check?'

'No, no. Let's just sit quietly for a moment and see if our mystery caller appears.'

'Why don't we just go in?'

'Because,' said Munro, craning his neck to face the house, 'there's a light on upstairs and we have no idea who it is. They could be dangerous.'

'Fair enough, although, I have to say, it's more than likely the cleaner or someone who's parked there to avoid getting a ticket.'

'Both possible scenarios, Charlie, but with limited probability. You see, Nick doesnae have a cleaner and there are no parking restrictions on this street. I'd say it's someone he knows.'

'What makes you so sure?'

'Because they're just leaving.'

* * *

Connolly carefully locked the front door, glanced up and down the street and, assuming she was quite alone, turned for the car. She stopped, startled at the sight of Munro and West ambling up the drive. Her grip tightened on the hold-all in her left hand.

'Well, well, well, this is a pleasant surprise,' said Munro.

'What are you doing here?' said Connolly, scowling.

'I could ask you the same question, tell you what, you go first.'

'It's none of your business.'

'Oh, but it is, Miss Connolly. Your bag seems awful heavy, would you like some help?'

'No. I can manage, it's not heavy,' said Connolly, 'it's just … just a few things for Nick. You know, clothes, toiletries…'

'Is that so?' said Munro. 'You'll not mind if we take a wee look, then?'

'I would mind; I'd mind very much. Now, if you'll excuse me, I have to…'

'Is this your vehicle, Miss Connolly?' said West.

'Aye, what of it?'

'Front nearside tyre. Bald.'

'So?'

'That's an offence,' said West.

'So's harassing innocent folk going about their business.'

'Have you got a valid driving licence, and insurance?'

'Of course,' said Connolly, 'what do you take me for?'

'Good, wait there a moment, would you. I'm just going to check.'

'Wait, hold on, it's, er, it's not mine. I borrowed it.'

'Really?' said West. 'How convenient. Who from?'

'Fella, works in the bar.'

'Name?'

'Don't remember,' said Connolly.

'Okay, then I can find out for you, shan't be long.'

'Hold on, look, what do you want?'

'I've already told you, Miss Connolly,' said Munro, 'we

just want to see what's in the bag. If you dinnae want to show us here, then by all means bring it with you, it's my guess that in approximately three minutes, we'll be taking you in for driving whilst uninsured, not to mention…'

Connolly dropped the bag on the ground and held her arms aloft.

'Go ahead,' she said, defiantly, 'I've nothing to hide, I've done nothing wrong.'

Munro heaved the bag onto the bonnet of the car and slowly unzipped it.

'My, my,' he said, 'you could buy yourself a new motor car with this lot.'

'Aye, maybe I will,' said Connolly. 'Look, it's all legit, it's Nick's money, from his aunty, the one who died, it's not as though…'

'Are you fond of game shows, Miss Connolly?' said Munro as he closed the bag.

'What?'

'You know, on the telly, the kind where they ask you a question, then give you a choice of answers?'

'Aye, maybe, what are you…'

'Here's one for you. If Sergeant West were to arrest you, would it be for: A, theft; B, handling stolen property; or C, being an accessory after the fact?'

'You're barking; you know that? Mental, off your head.'

'Actually, it's a trick question. The answer is: all three.'

Chapter 24

After hours, with its tables stripped of their starched, linen coverings and token vases of freshly-cut flowers, the hotel restaurant had all the ambience of a canteen on an industrial estate.

'Good job you booked,' said West dryly, as they sat sharing a bottle of red over a takeaway fish supper, 'otherwise we'd have never got in.'

'Pays to know the right people, Charlie. It's what you call *influence*. Aye, that's the word. Influence.'

'For some reason, it always tastes better out of the paper, than on a plate.'

'That's depends on the paper,' said Munro, 'you'd not be saying that if Tony Blair was peeking out from under your haddock.'

West laid down her fork, cradled her glass in both hands and stared wistfully into space.

'What is it, lassie?' said Munro.

'I don't know, it's just frustrating, that's all, I mean we're so close, and yet…'

'Och, cheer up, Charlie, it's not that bad, we've more in the bag than a sniper on a pheasant shoot, and as soon as we hear from the…'

Munro paused as the door swung open and the familiar, yet unexpected, clatter of stiletto heels on the wooden floor interrupted their conversation.

'My, my, this is cosy,' said Crawford sarcastically, as she swaggered towards them. 'Sergeant Campbell said I'd find you here. Thought you'd be in the bar.'

'We've not long finished, Isobel,' said Munro, 'fancy a chip?'

'I'll pass, thanks, chips aren't exactly my...'

'Perhaps, if you thought of them as *pommes frites*, they might seem a wee bit more ... inviting.'

'I think not,' said Crawford, sitting with a sigh and a rubbing her forehead as though troubled by a minor headache. 'Look, I haven't trudged all the way over here for nothing, there's something ... there's something you need to...'

'Before you go on,' said West, 'we've just charged Connolly, found her with a bag full of cash.'

'Cash?' said Crawford. 'You mean the money Nick...'

'Aye, right enough,' said Munro, 'so, tomorrow, all we have to do is file the report and wait for the results from...'

'I'm afraid that won't be possible, James.'

Munro, sensing something awry, glanced at West and took a slug of wine.

'And that would be, why exactly?' he said, bracing himself.

'Hourigan. Jack Hourigan,' said Crawford, avoiding eye contact. 'He's arriving a day early. Tomorrow. And I ... I can't afford to have you here. Either of you.'

'So, what you're saying is...?'

'What I'm saying is, you're off the case. As of now. End of.'

'You are joking?' said West, smarting as though she'd been slapped in the face. 'Tell me you're bloody joking. After all we've ... do you realise just how close we are to...'

'Yes, yes, Sergeant, I'm sure you are, but there's nothing I can do, I simply can't afford to take the risk. Look, if Hourigan gets wind of what's been going on, if he finds out I authorised the two of you to investigate the case instead of giving it to Greenock, he'll have my guts for garters.'

West sat back and glared at Munro, willing him to say something.

'Hold on,' she said, 'there's no need to chuck the baby out with the bath water, there is another way; we can work from the hotel, we don't even have to be in the bloody office.'

'Listen,' said Crawford, agitated by West's persistence, 'Hourigan is a pain in the arse, the only reason he's here is because they can't stand him down in Motherwell and, given half a chance, he'll go running straight to the top citing improper procedure, abuse of authority, anything he can think of, and I will be hauled over the coals. I shudder to think what they'll do to you. No. I'm sorry. That's it.'

'But…'

'No! I'll inform C.I.D. first thing. Naturally, I expect you to hand over everything you have pertaining to the investigation.'

Crawford flinched as Munro slowly turned to face her, his eyes cold and hard.

'There is nothing to hand over, Isobel,' he said, his voice slow and menacing, 'it's all on the computer, and you have copies of everything.'

'Right. Okay. Good,' said Crawford. 'Well, I suppose that's that then. Oh, don't look at me like that, you can see I have no choice, can't you?'

'Que sera, sera,' said Munro, 'perhaps we'll see you in the morning. I take it you'll not be stopping us from collecting a few items of a personal nature?'

'No, of course not. For chrissakes, James, I don't want this to end on a sour note. Maybe once this has all blown over, once C.I.D. have … you know, maybe we could…'

'Aye, maybe we could, Isobel. Maybe we could.'

West stared in disbelief as a downcast Crawford trudged towards the door, stopped abruptly, then turned and marched back to the table.

'I'm doing this as a courtesy James,' she said, producing a sealed envelope from her shoulder bag, 'Constable Reid asked me to give you this. If it's something you can…'

Munro, recognising immediately the monogrammed label overwritten in blue ink, uncharacteristically snatched it from her hands, tore it open and hastily flicked through the contents.

'Isobel,' he said, passing it to West as he stood and pulled on his coat, 'your decision-making may leave a bit to be desired, but you were right about one thing.'

'What's that?' said Crawford as they left her standing alone and confused.

'Case closed,' said Munro. 'End of.'

Chapter 25

The moon, set against a clear night sky peppered with stars, cast a bright, silvery wash over Dunmore House, rendering the lights along the drive superfluous. Munro killed the engine and sat silently as West, awestruck, watched a red vixen scamper across the lawn on a quest for food.

'Magical,' she whispered, 'so much nicer seeing them in the wild than foraging through the bin bags on the high street for a piece of KFC.'

'Well, someone's got to eat it, lassie,' said Munro, 'I'm just glad it's not me.'

West turned to face him.

'The Fiscal,' she said, 'I can't believe she kicked us out just because some overgrown parking attendant's coming up from the city.'

'Och, I know it's annoying, Charlie, but you cannae blame her, she's just covering her back. Dinnae forget, thanks to Nick, it was she who bent the rules to get us involved in the first place.'

'Yeah, I suppose you're right. At least she was good enough to show us the report.'

'Aye. And now we've got all we need, shall we?'

* * *

Fraser, wary of receiving visitors after nightfall, did not heave the door open with her usual aplomb, instead, she eased it ajar, just a couple inches, just enough to ascertain who the callers might be. Despite the look of relief on her face, she seemed, thought West, perturbed. Her smile was strained; her body, tense; her eyes, not too keen on making contact with hers.

'Apologies for the untimely intrusion, Mrs. Fraser,' said Munro, 'but it's important. We wouldnae be here otherwise, you know that, don't you?'

'Of course,' said Fraser, diffidently, 'it's quite alright.'

'You're sure, now? We're not keeping you from your bed, are we?'

'Och no, it's early yet. Now, in you come. Will I fetch you something? Tea perhaps, or a wee drop of…'

'No, no, you're alright,' said Munro, closing the door behind him and unzipping his jacket, 'very kind, but we'll not keep you long.'

Fraser cocked her head to one side and regarded Munro with a frown.

'You don't seem your usual self, Inspector,' she said, 'have you left that charming smile of yours in the motor car?'

'I'm afraid this is quite serious, Mrs. Fraser. If I wore a smile, I'd have to book myself for deception.'

'Well, in that case, you'd best go through, have yourself a seat.'

Munro, hands clasped behind his back, paced slowly back and forth until Fraser, clearly unsettled by his demeanour, joined West on the sofa.

'I'll not beat around the bush, Mrs. Fraser,' he said, turning to face her, 'did you know Freida had a Will?'

'I'm sorry?'

'A Last Will and Testament?'

'Well, I…'

'Did she ever discuss with it you?'

197

'I'm sorry, Inspector, but I don't quite see…'

'Mrs. Fraser,' said Munro, sternly, 'I'm sorry if I sound, brusque, impatient even, but if you're not willing to…'

'Yes, yes, alright. She did discuss it.'

'What, exactly?'

'Well,' said Fraser hesitantly, 'it was more of a joke, really. We joked about it. She said, if she goes first, I'll have nothing to worry about, that I'd be well looked after. And I'd say, if I went first, she'd get nothing.'

'And?'

'And what? That was it. I'd tell her to stop being so morbid. That I didn't want her money.'

'You didn't want her money?' said Munro.

'Well, no…'

'Why do you think she wanted to leave it to you?' said West. 'And not her sister perhaps? Or her daughter?'

'I don't know, Sergeant, all I know is, she said … she said she was depressed about her relationship with her daughter, called her selfish and greedy. A scrounger and a gold digger. She told me she'd rather leave it to someone more deserving, someone who'd enjoy it, not squander it. Someone who'd loved her for who she was. Anyway, what does it matter? I doubt she even went through with it.'

'Are you sure about that?' said Munro.

'Yes, of course,' said Fraser, bewildered, 'it was small talk between friends, why do you ask?'

'Because, Mrs. Fraser, Freida changed her Will just two days before she died, and she made you the main beneficiary.'

Fraser, wide-eyed, regarded Munro, then West, with a look of astonishment.

'Well, goodness me,' she said, patting her chest, 'I really don't what to say.'

Munro, eking out an excruciating pause, turned and strode purposefully towards the fireplace.

'You never did get over Donald, did you Mrs. Fraser?'

he said, throwing her off guard.

'Donald?'

'You and he, you were quite the lovebirds, once upon a time, were you not?'

'Me and…? Utter pish,' said Fraser, surprised, 'I've never heard such…'

'Mrs. Fraser,' said Munro slowly, as he glared at her, 'I've spoken with Mr. Reid. He's told me about your, relationship.'

Fraser blanched.

'I imagine you were quite distraught when he left you to marry somebody else. Aye, of course you were, it's only natural, but you muddled through, you managed to cope. In fact, even the arrival of a wee bairn, young Duncan there, couldnae keep you away. As long as you could see him, talk to him, have a wee drink maybe, it meant you had hope. Is that not right? Good. But there was one thing you couldnae cope with, Mrs. Fraser. One thing you simply could not abide, and that was the fact that, after all these years, your best friend, someone you trusted implicitly, was having an affair with him. Right under your nose.'

Fraser, in an effort to assert herself, stood abruptly.

'I need a sherry,' she said stoically, 'can I interest either of you in a glass?'

West declined politely as Munro waited for her to return to her seat. He stood, motionless, and watched as she sipped her sherry, then downed it in one.

'See, here, Mrs. Fraser,' he said, staring at the floor, 'here's the thing. I think you knew Freida had changed her Will, and I think you knew she'd made you the main beneficiary, but, I don't believe she did it out of the kindness of heart, or because she held you in such high regard. She did it because you told her to. You blackmailed her. You threatened to tell Mrs. Reid about Freida's affair with her husband, knowing full well that such a revelation would have blown them apart. Can you imagine the consequences? Can you imagine just how devastated that family would have been? Dear, dear, especially young Duncan. It would have ruined his career in the force, I mean, imagine the papers, in a town like this, they'd have had a field day. But you know Freida, Mrs. Fraser, generous to a fault. Never put herself first. So, she gave in to your demand, and she changed her Will, simply to protect Donald's family. Now, would you say I'm right, or thereabouts?'

West held her breath for fear of breaking the silence whilst Fraser, not daring to look up, hung her head and nodded.

'Good,' said Munro, startling them both as he clapped his hands, 'let's move on, then. Next item on the agenda.'

'Next item?' said Fraser, almost quivering with shock. 'You mean there's more?'

'Oh, aye,' said Munro, grinning, 'lots more. You see, the main reason we're here, Mrs. Fraser, is to give you some good news. I'm sure you'll be glad to know, we've caught the person responsible for Freida's death.'

Fraser fell back in her seat, sighing as though a weight had been lifted from her shoulders.

'Well, thank goodness for that,' she said, 'thank goodness. I hope they get what they deserve. Perhaps now she can be laid to rest.'

'Aye, that she can,' said Munro, 'that, she can.'

'I don't know about you, but I could do with another drink,' said Fraser, passing the empty glass to West, 'would you mind, dear?'

West duly obliged and recharged her glass.

'Now,' said Munro, 'to continue. Mrs. Fraser, you remember those chaps from forensics? The gentlemen who took all those bits and bobs from Freida's kitchen, you know, the glasses and the wine bottles and…?'

'Och, yes. Very polite they were. Didnae say very much, though.'

'No, I doubt they did. Probably concentrating on their work. Anyway, they analysed everything they took away, ran all sorts of clever, wee, scientific tests, and they came back with some interesting results.'

'Really?'

'Oh aye,' said Munro. 'for example, did you know, one of those bottles was contaminated with anti-freeze?'

'Anti-freeze?' said Fraser, puzzled.

'Aye, would you believe it? Anti-freeze. I never knew anti-freeze was poisonous, but, if administered correctly, say, mixed with alcohol, you cannae even taste it. You cannae taste a thing, but, a day or so later, well, job done, as they say.'

'Well, I never.'

'Interesting, is it not?' said Munro. 'So's this. Remember the wine Nick brought for Freida?'

'Yes, I do,' said Fraser, smiling, 'the Riesling, och, and it was open! The bottle was open. You don't mean...? Surely not? Not young Nick, dear God, how could he ... why on earth would he...?'

'Hold on there, Mrs. Fraser, hold on, now,' said Munro. 'You're very good, but you'll not be nominated for an Oscar anytime soon.'

Fraser, scratching nervously at the empty glass with her nails, glanced at West.

'I'm sorry, Inspector?' she said, quietly. 'What do you mean?'

'The bottle of Riesling was clean. There was nothing wrong with it, same with the Tempranillo, but you knew that already, didn't you? It was the other bottle that was contaminated. The bottle of Pinot Grigio. The Pinot you bought for Freida.'

'Patience is a virtue, Mrs. Fraser,' said West, standing, 'if you hadn't been so hasty, you'd have got your money, eventually.'

Epilogue

With the regatta due to start in less than twelve hours, and every hotel and bed and breakfast booked solid for the next fortnight, parking anywhere in Inverkip had suddenly become worse than trying to find a space in a multi-storey on Black Friday. This left Munro with no option but to park his car on the verge, where it would no doubt be ticketed by sunrise, and walk the 500 yards back to the hotel.

'Snifter?' said West, turning her collar up against the cold, night air. 'Bar's still open.'

'No, no, it's late,' said Munro, 'well, perhaps just a wee one.'

'Who'd have thought, eh? Mrs. Fraser, of all people. Dear old, kind, sweet, friendly, Mrs. Fraser. She seemed so nice, like…'

'Like butter wouldn't melt?' said Munro. 'There's a reason for that, Charlie, she's as cold as ice.'

'Have you told Isobel?' said West, smiling.

'Aye,' said Munro, 'well, she wasnae there, I left her a message. I told her Fraser's been charged, she's being held in custody, and the report's on what used to be my desk. She can pick it up tomorrow.'

West drove her hands deep into her pockets and shrugged off a shiver.

'There's something quite forlorn about her,' she said, 'downtrodden. Don't you think?'

'Who? Isobel? Och, she's just lonely,' said Munro, 'she'll find someone, soon enough.'

'She's still got the hots for you.'

'Aye, and I'm not in the market for getting burned.'

'Why don't you have lunch with her?'

'I'll not lead her on, Charlie, I'm spoken for. Don't get me wrong, I'm a compassionate fellow, charitable even, but I'm not a masochist.'

'So, what happens now?' said West with a sigh.

'All back to normal,' said Munro, 'no doubt you'll be heading back south, pick up where you left off?'

'Maybe,' said West.

'Maybe? Are you not missing your home? Your wee flat and all your pals?'

'To be honest, no. Not really.'

'Och, see here Charlie,' said Munro, 'it's just like coming back off your holidays, once you're back in the swing, you'll be fine.'

'Yeah, suppose so.'

'Trust me, if I know you, and I do, it'll not be long before you make D.I.'

'Maybe,' said West, 'but, the thing is, I quite…'

West paused as they reached the hotel.

'Quite what?' said Munro.

'Oh, nothing,' said West, 'forget about it.'

'No, no, go on, let's hear it.'

'I'm just not sure I'm ready for it. I like it here, it's slower than London, easier on the eye, less aggression. Oh, I don't know, people just seem to smile more.'

'Aye, right enough,' said Munro, laughing, 'although that's probably because they've just had a win at the bookies.'

West said nothing, smiled softly and pushed open the

door.

'Are you familiar with the concept of gardening?' said Munro, holding back.

'Sorry?'

'The planting of flowers, shrubs and trees, to create an outdoor space where one might like to … linger?'

'I've never tried. Why?'

'Well, I've a garden to sort out, I promised Jean I'd do it once this case was closed. If you're not in a hurry to go home, I've a spare room, not very big, but adequate enough. You're welcome to stay a while, if you like.'

'Really?' said West. 'With you? Are you sure?'

'Och, you'd be doing me a favour, really. I could use the company. To be honest, it can get a wee bit…'

'I think I'd like that. I think I'd like that, a lot.'

'Aye, you probably will, Charlie. You probably will.'

Character List

D.I. JAMES MUNRO - Shrewd, smart and cynical with an inability to embrace retirement, he has a knack for expecting the unexpected.

D.S. CHARLOTTE WEST - Racked with self-doubt after a floundering engagement, she regains her confidence with Munro as her mentor in his native Scotland.

D.C.I. NICK McGREEVY - Prefers life off the straight and narrow and reaping the rewards of an unethical approach to policing.

SERGEANT IAIN CAMPBELL - Content in his work and happiest with a pint, the only thing missing in his life is a woman.

CONSTABLE DUNCAN REID - As keen as mustard with a sideways sense of humour, he has a burning desire to work his way up the ranks and join the drugs squad.

ISOBEL CRAWFORD (PROCURATOR FISCAL) - Sassy, sexy and single who likes her men as robust and as complex as an oak-aged Rioja.

RUDY KAPPELHOFF - A post-war immigrant from Schleswig-Holstein whose unexpected divorce made his work ethic as tough as the boots he repairs for a living.

FREIDA KAPPELHOFF - A single divorcee who still carries a torch for her ex but refuses to let him know.

CALLUM McKENZIE - Ex-teacher and philanderer with a torrid past who enjoyed a relationship with Freida Kappelhoff before and after her divorce.

LORNA McKENZIE - Unsure about her parentage and disturbed by her father's activities, lives on benefits and the immoral earnings of her boyfriend.

MRS. FRASER - A lifelong spinster, she is a friend and confident to Freida Kappelhoff whose looks and lifestyle she secretly covets.

If you enjoyed this book, please let others know by leaving a quick review on Amazon. Also, if you spot anything untoward in the paperback, get in touch. We strive for the best quality and appreciate reader feedback.

editor@thebookfolks.com

www.thebookfolks.com

ALSO BY PETE BRASSETT

In this series:

SHE – book 1
ENMITY – book 3
DUPLICITY – book 4
TERMINUS – book 5
TALION – book 6
PERDITION – book 7

Other titles:

THE WILDER SIDE OF CHAOS
YELLOW MAN
CLAM CHOWDER AT LAFAYETTE AND SPRING
THE GIRL FROM KILKENNY
BROWN BREAD
PRAYER FOR THE DYING
KISS THE GIRLS

Made in the USA
Middletown, DE
04 May 2019